AMANDA

The exciting scent of jasmine and roses aroused his senses. He desperately craved her soft lips, anxious to sample the sweet nectar stored inside her mouth, but found the kiss was a whispered gift against his slightly damp forehead. He realized his fantasies were becoming more foe than friend when it came to Amanda Wyatt.

* * *

She looked at her hand, remembering the strength of his callused fingers as they curled around hers, pressing them against the dark mat of hair that furred his chest. . . . Idly, she wondered what he would be like as a lover. Slow and thoughtful, patient and tender? Or would he be wild and rough, quick and selfish? Somehow, both appealed. . . .

Other Books in the
Finding Mr. Right Series

PAPER TIGER *by Elizabeth Neff Walker*
DANCING SEASON *by Carla A. Neggers*

Coming Soon

LOVE FOR THE TAKING *by Beth Christopher*

FINDING
MR. RIGHT

BEST LAID PLANS

ELAINE RACO CHASE

AVON
PUBLISHERS OF BARD, CAMELOT, DISCUS AND FLARE BOOKS

BEST LAID PLANS is an original publication of Avon Books. This work has never before appeared in book form.

AVON BOOKS
A division of
The Hearst Corporation
959 Eighth Avenue
New York, New York 10019

First Avon Printing, April, 1983

AVON TRADEMARK REG. U. S. PAT. OFF. AND IN OTHER COUN-TRIES, MARCA REGISTRADA, HECHO EN U.S.A.

Printed in the U. S. A.

WFH   10   9   8   7   6   5   4   3   2   1

BEST LAID PLANS

Chapter One

THE COPPER-SHADED lectern light illuminated the script for that evening's fashion show. Amanda Wyatt's lucid gray eyes were fixed on the paper; her breathing had suddenly been reduced to shallow, jerky spasms. Words had been added and subtracted, transposed and re-created. Blue-pencil scribbles overpowered the once-neat typewritten page.

No matter how many times she had rearranged and rewritten her notes, the composition sounded—"Boring!" Amanda finally spoke the cursed word aloud. Again blue graphite was scrawled across the bond paper. She hoped a few clever adjectives and adverbs would inject much-needed vitality not only into the sentences but into their author as well.

The newly sharpened pencil point snapped. That sharp sound was accompanied by the fracturing of Amanda's composure. She hurled the pencil toward her nemesis—the runway. Watching the pencil fall to the floor far short of its goal, she snatched up her notes and proceeded to strangle them between cold, clammy fingers.

Arms crossed over full breasts, hands locked onto shoulders, Amanda buried her nose against skin that no longer smelled bath-powder fresh but musty and stale. *Now, now,* she gave herself a sharp mental directive, *this is no time for a temper tantrum.*

Taupe-tinted eyelids drifted closed. The blackness provided a soothing, albeit momentary respite from the frenzied activities in the ballroom. She wished it were as easy to shut her ears. The sounds of music, roaring vacuum

1

cleaners, clattering dishes, clanking silver and chattering, shouting busboys seemed magnified to nerve-fragmenting proportions.

Her fingers pressed deeper into red-suede-covered shoulders. Amanda had to stop herself from running away, will herself to ignore the icy fingers of dread that gripped her very soul. Chastising herself for feeling so helpless, she tried to look at the situation logically.

It was not as though this were her first fashion show. In fact, it was her third of the year—she had managed eight such charity events in the past sixteen months. Each one had been more successful than the last. First-night jitters had no place here. *But how many jitters were really due to the show?* prodded an inner devil that had manifested itself in her mind.

Amanda shook her head to clear it and forced her attention back to the dress rehearsal. She was surprised to find the runway unoccupied. She cued outfit number seventeen. No one appeared. "Seventeen! Lizette! Where the hell is Lizette?" Her normally well-modulated soprano splintered in a frantic appeal.

"Seventeen?" Amanda shouted into the podium's microphone. The response was the crash of metal chairs against the wooden stage floor. A frustrated groan escaped between clenched teeth. After counting to ten, Amanda spoke in a more subdued tone. "Bianca, please find Lizette." A hand pushed apart the emerald stage curtains and gave her a complying wave.

Her Aries horoscope in this morning's *Times-Picayune* had warned that today would be eventful. Amanda wondered why her ruling planet, Mars, couldn't make the scheduled events orderly and calm. Why did she have to battle not only her own frustrations but those of everyone else as well?

A wry smile twisted her ginger-glossed lips. But wasn't her real problem the fact that everything was in the proverbial apple-pie order? Every waking hour was relegated to a pigeonhole existence. Wasn't that the real crux of her listlessness and depression?

Her thoughts drifted and darted to the three seasons she had spent as chief designer on Seventh Avenue. She had been scared to death at the unveiling of each collection. Indigestion, insomnia and headaches were all routine companions of her sixteen-hour workdays. Yet that anxiety and fear had nourished her like no other food.

She must be a masochist to wish for the challenge of the old days. There had always been something going wrong, but she had loved it. Fashion! Laughter bubbled, then died in her throat. It was glamorous and boring, underrated and overrated, satisfying and painful, exasperating and exciting, unpredictable and yet somehow the same. For all that, Amanda had never been able to break free. She was a willing prisoner, loving the power, prestige and trauma this profession fed to her soul.

The ornate wall clock was a silent but obvious reminder that in four hours this rehearsal would turn into the main event. "Seventeen." She again barked the order into the microphone. Amanda's gray eyes surveyed the model who finally appeared center stage. Lizette pranced down the runway, a trail of curlers plopping and bouncing in her wake. The strawberry yogurt Amanda had gulped in lieu of lunch began to burn its way up her esophagus.

"Damn it, Lizette, look alive!" Her voice crackled and spluttered, then the microphone died. "Do it again." Her fist made a series of circular motions above her head; the blatant physical gesture triumphed over the noise level in the ballroom.

Lizette's myopic hazel eyes squinted at the blurred movement, then rolled heavenward in mute understanding. *Wasn't this woman ever satisfied? She's been a bitch all morning.* Pursing full mauve lips, the model carelessly slumped back toward the stage, then disappeared between the velvet curtains that cloaked the wings.

Amanda turned and repeated the signaled instructions for Isaac Bevans at the special-effects console. His Afro bobbed as he nodded his understanding. "Once more with feelin', baby," he crooned, wiggling slim, denim-clad hips into a more comfortable position on the padded stool.

Isaac's competent fingers moved swiftly among the sliders and audio pots. He deftly recued the sound track while simultaneously reprogramming the sequential footlights.

At Amanda's direction it all started again. Piano, string bass and drums created a syncopated rhythm that filled the auditorium. Strobelike frosted bulbs that edged the stage and runway visually defined the throbbing jazz melody.

Lizette appeared, haloed in a shimmering pink spotlight. She moved center stage, then dutifully turned and twirled her way down the beige carpet runner. The bored expression on her cosmetic sculptured face matched her perfunctory movements.

"Double damn that girl," Amanda cursed again. "You'd think she was wearing a feedbag instead of a Dior." Her narrowed gray eyes followed the model's listless movements.

Lizette was supposed to be a pro. She was certainly paid well to display her gaunt body with elegance and grace. Emitting a throaty groan, Amanda wondered where all the model's professionalism was hiding.

Curved like elegant talons, Amanda's fingers clamped on either side of her head. Her brick-red nails vented a frenzy of pent-up frustrations against short copper-brown curls. What was the problem? Had her own ennui been transmitted to everyone involved with this show?

The models had no right to act this way. Damn them! They were humored and coddled. They were draped in originals, pampered by cosmetic artists, coiffured in elegance and enhanced with real jewels. No fakes. No seconds. No copies. Only the best.

In the beginning the best had been enough. Energy levels had been high, and each show was more intoxicating than the last. But January's resort and cruise wear for the Heart Fund had failed to dissipate the postholiday blues. And, while February's Mardi Gras gala boosted the United Fund, it generated only a modicum of stimulation that apparently was quite short-lived.

March proved to be a rude lion as it snarled out across

the South. But inside the Hyatt Ballroom, magnificent crystal chandeliers presided like miniature suns radiating down on lacy gazebos, bubbling fountains and garden walkways populated by scarlet tulips, yellow daffodils, white daisies and lush greenery.

While Mother Nature had made umbrellas, slickers and boots *de rigueur* for the past ten days, spectacular summer wear in bold, bright colors and styles waited temptingly on dressing-room racks. Yet for all the emotion the models were exhibiting, Amanda felt she could have used the mannequins that graced her shop on Royal Street.

Head bowed, she began to massage the stiffness from her neck. Inhaling and exhaling three times, Amanda told herself to relax, to remain calm. Hadn't she met and conquered worse challenges than this? But the tension was still there, hidden not only in the constricted highway of tendons on her neck but straining every muscle in her body. Willpower and words—today they proved poor tranquilizers.

Lizette's final pirouette made Amanda wince. New Orleans' black-tie audience wasn't paying one hundred fifty dollars a person to the Cancer Society to view this blasé performance. An awful thought nagged at her. Perhaps *she* had unconsciously trampled everyone's enthusiasm. Guilt smothered her. The real stars of the fashion show were the designs. Homage *had* to be paid to these creations. These fabric children—conceived with love, cut and sewn with tenderness and sent out into the world with hope and fear.

Resentment at her own loss of faith was all-consuming; adrenaline and anger overcame her inertia. Amanda's long, dark-stockinged legs dismissed the four steps to the runway in two graceful leaps. She caught Lizette by the shoulders and spun her around. Even, white teeth smiled at the startled young woman, but the smile did not reach her glinting eyes. "This is silk, Lizette, painstakingly sewn by hand in crowded workrooms by at least twenty skilled seamstresses." Amanda's expert fingers gently readjusted the shoulders on the red and white dress accented with bold purple stripes.

"This is a masterpiece," she continued, impersonally smoothing the horizontal bodice over the model's minuscule breasts, "worked on for weeks and weeks, and"—her flintlike gaze bored into Lizette's blinking hazel eyes—"in less than two minutes, on your body, it is either condemned or adored."

Dropping to her knees, Amanda straightened a rope of amethyst ribbons that circled a waist no bigger than a double handspan. "You are wearing art, Lizette, *couturier*'s art. Dior was awarded the Legion of Honor for his designs." She looked up from repinning the hem. "In Paris this dress is considered a national treasure."

Amanda nodded with satisfaction at her adjustments, then dexterously returned to her feet, towering over the young woman. "This is what dreams are made of, and you are the keeper of this dream. Tonight you are the owner of this luxury." Her voice grew as passionate as her words. The stern lines that had hardened her attractive features disappeared. She bloomed with the intensity of her emotions. "Silk, Lizette, feel it. It gets better, softer, more sensuous every time you wear it."

Wide, almond eyes glowed like polished solitaires. "Let this luxury show on your face. Feel it caress your body." Her long fingers re-formed the black strands that had escaped Lizette's curlers. "Make this dress your lover and return the passion."

Her peripheral gaze caught the other models clustered in the wings. "Come out, ladies!" Amanda motioned them to assemble onstage. "I want to see and feel the opulence, the glamour, the spirit. Look out there." A slender wrist directed attention toward their splendorous surroundings. "We've created a dream and made you the stars. You command the attention. You are the epitome of fashion."

She took time to inspect each model, making small adjustments to shoulders or wrists, reangling a straw hat or straightening a belt. "I want you to become a part of what you're wearing. Feel the fabrics, drink in the textures, spin your own fantasies. Listen and move with the music. It's intoxicating."

Amanda clapped her hands. "Now let me experience these masterpieces." Her attitude was light but there was a sharp insistence in her tone. "Excite this room. Dazzle these people. Make them stand and beg for an encore." Her voice lowered persuasively. "Release the ecstasy hidden in your soul."

She turned and walked the length of the runway, instinctively aware that her own regal carriage and supple stride were under close scrutiny. "Harry!" Amanda shouted, lifting her hand toward the balcony. "Give me a blue filter for the first three, then blend in the pink." A shadowy figure immediately made the transition. She signaled Isaac, and the music cued Lizette.

The improvement was as dramatic as the fashions. Models turned into dancers, and dancers turned into ballerinas. It was a well-orchestrated symmetry that enhanced the clothes.

The dulcet chords of Count Basie's "The Lady Is a Tramp" emphasized the contrast in daytime fashions. European and American designers had captured the independent woman. The contemporary woman would not be forced into one shape; she would choose from an enormous variety of silhouettes and styles. The clothes were marvelous, Amanda thought; Basile's lean white linen and ballooning culottes; Fendi's sensuous suede gauchos and toga-tunic pants; Versace's petal shorts peeping beneath a kimono coat; Ungaro's blossoming chemise and Feraud's striped silk culottes.

Clarinets, horns and saxophones wailed to herald the transition into evening wear. Crisp agility sparked Dior's pleated and ruffled taffeta, while Yves St. Laurent's scarlet toga slithered with insinuating bareness. Chanel's paillette embroidery floated like a virginal maiden in contrast to Oscar de la Renta's rich, turquoise, bead-encrusted harem treasure. Givenchys that plunged to the navel or ruffled to the chin were displayed with artistic flair.

Halston's bugle-beaded organza swept by, to be immediately replaced by a strapless Nipon taffeta ball gown. Adele Simpson's boldly striped tunic and trousers was followed by Geoffrey Beene's multicolored obi-wrapped gown. Harem dressing in red from Mary McFadden and drop-dead glamorous tunics from Michaele Vollbracht fluttered like graceful butterflies. Tarquin's ruched crepe and magenta marabou spun toward the stage wings chased by Ralph Lauren's prairie plaid.

Amanda's smile broadened with each new display. Her energy level was as puffed as Adolfo's candy-cane-striped gown and as effervescent as Bill Blass's champagne taffeta bubble. Enthusiasm turned into applause and when the last trumpet note faded, Amanda's own appreciation was echoed by the workers in the ballroom.

"That was perfect! Just beautiful, everyone!" She continued applauding until the models joined her onstage. "You've captivated and charmed them. I am very pleased with you all." Amanda turned a more sober countenance to the petite, gray-haired woman who stood at her side. "Any problems, Bianca?"

"A few, some tempers but—" Mme. Dupree gave a futile shrug. Two slender fingers came up to massage a sunken temple. "The Lanvin on Felicia is very snug." She nodded toward a delicate blue and white cotton. "Too many"—she hunted for the proper English word—"pastries." A scolding finger wagged at the willowy blonde chattering in line. "I will release it. The changing will go faster, yes?"

"Yes," Amanda agreed, her critical gaze judging the strain on the puffed-sleeve, square-necked bodice. "What an improvement—don't you agree?"

"Very"—Bianca's gold crown glinted among worn, yellow teeth—"magnificent." Dark blue eyes cast a direct stare at Amanda, widening at the latter's sallow complexion and weary features. "What about you?" The words came out a mixture of French and stammered English.

"I, too, will be *magnificent* if they perform this well tonight," Amanda assured the aged woman. She gave Bianca's rounded shoulders a companionable hug. "This will be our last show until August. The charity tennis and golf competitions will replace us in a few more weeks."

Mme. Dupree drew a grateful breath. "The rest will be most welcome." Her skilled fingers were busy regrouping the slender dressmaker's pins in the cushion snapped around her wrist. "Your gown is ready. I lowered the straps, pressed it and sent it up to the hotel chamber."

"What would I do without you, Bianca?" Amanda smiled her appreciation. She felt gray eyes grow suspiciously moist as they focused on the wiry French seamstress who had been in her employ for the past four years. "We've made quite a team, yes?"

"But of course, my little one."

An airy chuckle replaced Amanda's momentary slide into nostalgia. Bianca Dupree had been calling her "little one" since their first meeting. The endearment had always amused her, considering *petite* was an imposing seventy inches. "All right, ladies." Amanda clapped for order. "Next is the lingerie. This will be fun."

Her easy smile encompassed the attentive group. "Silks and satins and lace and ruffles provide instant fantasies. Think Hollywood. Silver screen. Arabian sheiks. Folies-Bergère." Amanda was laughing, but a red-tinted fingernail stabbed the air with a distinct warning. "Isaac's spliced together a Duke Ellington trio that's a perfect introduction for this line. I want you to seduce the audience, make them desert Jean-Claude's fabulous cuisine to stare at you in rapturous delight."

She spoke again to Bianca. "You'll have ten minutes to exchange the gowns for the lingerie. Mr. Cramer will be giving a slide presentation on the new cancer research wing while the busboys are picking up the dinner plates and the waiters are bringing the *crème brûlée* and *pousse-café*."

"It seems I am the preparer of the *pièces de résistance*." Mme. Dupree's mouth formed a tight *moue;* the vertical lines that surrounded her thin, waxen lips deepened in distaste.

"Our seductive fashions were selected to rival the dessert," Amanda returned on a wry note. "We must give the audience a finale worth their donation, *my dear.*" She favored the seamstress with an audacious wink.

Mme. Dupree muttered something Amanda had once read scrawled on a curb in Paris and turned away. "Hurry! Hurry!" Bianca's pink-smocked figure herded the giggling young women backstage to the dressing room.

"Oh, Miss Wyatt."

"Yes, Isaac." Amanda stepped to the edge of the runway. "Is there a problem with the slides?"

"No, ma'am." He shook his head, index finger pushing the aviator-style sunglasses tight against the bridge of his nose. "I'm going to run through them right now and then I'll fix your mike." Isaac held up a white telephone receiver. "There's a call for you."

"Thanks." Sliding the Princess phone against her ear, Amanda found only a dial tone to greet her. "Did you catch who it was?"

"Your shop," he related, dark brows rising in satisfaction as the remote-control device expertly lowered the projection screen into position against the stage curtains. "I was holding that call for quite a while," Isaac announced, his talented fingers manipulating the machine controls.

Amanda's shapely shadow became silhouetted against a construction site while the slide projector showed the progress being made on the cancer research wing. After she dialed seven ingrained numbers, a melodic southern accent greeted her with: "Good afternoon, Rags 'n' Riches."

"Hi, Sherry. You called?"

"Hello, boss. How's everything?"

"I've got to rewrite that damn speech, and frankly both the troups and I could use some extra energy," came her caustic rejoiner. "What's happening there?"

"Good things to give you extra energy," Sherry said, laughing, her tone as effusive as a greeting card. "I poured iced lime-spiked mineral water into Mrs. Dowling all afternoon and she wrote out a check for a Mollie Parnis, an Anne Klein and half a dozen Pierre Cardin separates that just arrived. She'll be in Monday so Bianca can fit her."

"Leaving you in charge is certainly proving monetarily advantageous," Amanda agreed, her winsomeness belying the spasm that twisted the muscles in her shoulders. "Did you have any trouble with Reuben?"

"Not a bit," the assistant manager continued. "I dutifully listened to his gossipy *shmooz,* told him politely that his last runner ended up on the markdown rack and took a look at his sleeper."

Sherry took a deep breath. "Mandy, he has the most gorgeous silk T-shirts you've ever seen, expertly sewn, high-quality and a great price, so—" She coughed twice.

Amanda stopped exercising her back. "So you ordered them," she finished matter-of-factly.

"Well . . . Reuben said we were getting first look, the color selection was breathtaking and I know they'll be Fords," Sherry returned in a rapid staccato. "I . . . I didn't think a token order was out of line."

"It wasn't and neither were you." Amanda intuitively provided the words that would salve her assistant's conscience.

"Well, I just didn't want you to think . . . I mean, I really appreciate all the authority you've given me and . . . we . . ." Sherry stammered in nervous discomfort. "I've just loved working for you the past two years and I would never want to overstep my position," she finished on an apologetic, formal note.

"You work *with* me, Sherry Lau, not *for* me," Amanda corrected. Then a smile curved her full lips. "I'll let you know when you ever overstep your bounds."

Relieved laughter drifted through the phone lines. "Despite the rain, we had a marvelous day. Busy as hell and all the stock is moving. Oh, by the way, Mandy, you had a visitor about half an hour ago."

"Another salesman?"

"Attaché case not a sample bag. No, he was definitely not in the rag trade." A purely feminine giggle added credence to her statement. "Quiet and shy, big guy with dark hair and a moustache. Ve-rry attractive."

"That description does not ring any bells, although,"

11

her tongue clicked against the roof of her mouth, "you're making him sound most intriguing. Did he leave a card?"

"Uh-uh. We were swamped and when I went back to ask, he'd gone. Sorry."

Amanda's high forehead puckered in thoughtful contemplation. "I'll bet it was that insurance agent who's been trying to sell me an IRA. He loves being cryptic." Her smoky eyes were drawn to the wall clock. Father Time was showing no mercy. "Listen, Sherry, I've got to get the girls out for the finale. If everything is done, why don't you call it a day."

"Thanks," came an appreciative murmur. "Hey, have a little fun tonight. I'll open up tomorrow."

Fun. Amanda winced. Wasn't fun supposed to invigorate, not drain? Mentally chastising herself, she resolutely pushed aside the depressing devil that had pursued her for the past few months and plunged back into her work. "How did the slides time out, Isaac?" she inquired, handing back the long-corded receiver.

"If Mr. Cramer follows this speech," he tapped the blue index cards, "you'll have seventeen minutes. That includes getting the screen off the stage."

"Bianca will kiss you over the extra time." She smiled, then the curved lips drooped. "Let's hope the little darlings can do this in one delicately smooth take."

Isaac flashed her a wide-toothed grin. "I automatically reset the runway lights and switch to the red filaments." His large hands curved in a caressing gesture along the metal console housing. "That will warn and silence the audience for your opening lines, and then I'll fade up with the music."

"Sounds perfect. Let me see if they're set backstage. Maybe we can wrap this up fast and get in an hour's rest before the public comes sashaying in." Amanda made her way back to the velour-draped wings.

Mme. Dupree scurried past the glamorous queue poised for the finale. "Twelve minutes, good—yes?" Pale nails pointedly tapped the antique pocket watch suspended from a black ribbon around her thin, lined neck.

"Exceptional, but you won't have to rush." Amanda's comforting hand calmed Bianca's twitching, age-spotted fingers. "Isaac tells me you'll have another five minutes."

The sprightly *couturière* blew at a gray lock that evaded the pins holding her sleek chignon. "That will help, thank you." Bianca waved toward the nostalgic, ruffled petticoats steeped in lace. "Charming."

"Very," Amanda concurred, inspecting the collection of dainty confections that conjured romantic visions and hinted at more provocative nighttime intimacies. "They look adorable."

The initial offering started with a pristine eruption of Edwardian lawn ruffles, satin streamers on lacy camisoles, pastel teddys and precocious merry widows. Then came slithering, satiny forties pinup girl gowns, maraboued jackets and floaty pajamas. The climax was an all-out seduction made with the voyeur in mind. A true fantasy courtesy of the wizardry of metallic bras, sheer harem pants, sassy Parisienne teddys, plunging silk pajamas, clingy gowns and pantaloons. It was a baker's dozen that began with a look of innocence, sprinkled on a hint of coquetry and finished by captivating and enticing the imagination.

"You all look enchanting. I doubt one mouthful of dessert will be consumed when you step on the runway. All eyes will be devouring these luscious delights." Amanda's words inspired the preening group, but her clear gaze concentrated on Lizette.

The lead model looked every inch the Gibson Girl. Black hair in a billowing bubble, heart-shaped beauty mark pasted on her high, rouged cheekbone, her slim figure was now an hourglass in a pale lavender silk camisole and blousy, satin-trimmed bloomers.

Amanda knew if Lizette put a judicious jiggle in each step and a flirtatious smile on her face the other models would duplicate and embellish that effort. The girls were highly competitive, each eager to attain lead status and anxious to bathe their egos in applause.

"The music Isaac selected certainly fits this scintillating

lingerie," Amanda continued, her voice more authoritative. "Match the carefree lightness in 'Satin Doll,' slink into 'Body and Soul' and titillate with 'Walk on the Wild Side.'

"When Ellington's last piano note tinkles away, no one should want to go to heaven, just straight to the bedroom." She flashed them an unrepentant grin. Her hands clapped for order, trying to diffuse the giggles and laughter. "Let's do this in one—"

"Excuse me, Miss Wyatt." Isaac's palm cupped her elbow.

"Please don't say we have another problem," her suddenly weary voice begged.

"I'm not sure," he returned, thumb jerking back toward the ballroom. "There's a dude here insisting on seeing you. He pushed his way past the maître d'. He's not with the hotel or the Cancer Society." Isaac's baritone lowered another octave. "I stopped him just as he was heading up the runway."

"Dark hair and a moustache?" At his affirmative nod, Amanda's straight nose wrinkled. "It must be that pesky insurance man who was at the shop. What he won't do for a commission!"

Isaac flexed broad shoulders. "Hey, no sweat. I can bounce him easy." Pushing up the white sleeves on his knit shirt, he angled toward the stage staircase.

"Wait a minute." Amanda's voice halted the burly Tulane running back who also held a spot on the dean's list in engineering.

"Let me handle him." She gave Isaac an appreciative smile. "Who knows? He just may have a dynamite policy."

Her fingernail clicked against the glass face on Bianca's pocket watch. "Give me ten more minutes and then," her smoky gaze slanted at Isaac, "lower the lights and start that music."

He was seated at the corner tulip-bouqueted table, elbows on the green linen cloth, one charcoal slack-covered knee bouncing to an inner rhythm. The broad shoulders and back that confronted Amanda commanded attention. Smiling slightly, she knew exactly what was going to transpire. They would exchange the usual amenities, she'd take his card, shake his hand and give him a well-mannered, well-practiced version of: "Don't call me, I'll call you."

As her black leather pumps quietly traveled the thirty-foot carpeted runway, Amanda viewed her target with judicial appraisal. At least the man was impeccably groomed. She focused on his masculine silhouette, following the dark brown hair that waved and molded against his head before edging a crisp beige shirt collar. The tailoring on the blue-gray glen plaid blazer was meticulous, the blue-and-beige-accented fabric quite distinctive.

One well-shod foot echoed against the wooden step the same instant Amanda recognized the designer jacket was an Allyn St. George. The man stood and turned. Gray eyes collided with brown. He was no stranger.

She blinked twice. "Lucas?" The name was whispered, her memory questioned. Amanda stopped, cocked her head and stared. "Lucas!" She began to run, literally skidding to a halt in front of him.

The amber-flecked hazel eyes that surveyed her were familiar—as was the truant dark curl that insisted on falling against his broad forehead. Lines had etched his wide brow, crinkled the corners around his eyes, subtly aging his rugged, sun-bronzed features. The rangy, long-legged, loose-limbed body had filled out; the virile masculine physique was accented by the impeccably tailored clothes.

Amanda lifted her hand, a gentle forefinger examined the thick, dark moustache that shrouded his firm upper lip. "Lucas Crosse, whenever did you grow this?"

Pulling his head back, he lunged it forward and snapped at her finger like a turtle. "I thought it would toughen up this face. Give it that distinguished barrister look," Lucas explained in his best sanctimonious, courtroom manner. His own pomposity made him grin, and two dimples dented his lean cheeks, making a mockery of his officious tone.

"You look beautiful." Had it really been two years since he'd last seen her? Funny, whenever he opened her letters or heard her melodic voice on the phone, his mind replayed visual souvenirs. But the pictures weren't of this Amanda.

If anything, she was more attractive than he'd remembered. Her face had broadened, though the chin was still pointedly determined. Her eyes had always reminded him of the mist on a Highland moor—mysterious, patient, clouded with dreams. Today they sparked with flames, reflecting the red suede outfit that defined a more womanly anatomy.

Two large hands cupped her face before rumpling the nimbus of sienna curls. "Amanda Wyatt, whatever have you done to your hair?" Lucas' deep voice mimicked.

She wrinkled her pert nose. "It was a birthday present: to me from me. That midback braid suddenly got very heavy and old, so—" two fingers made a scissorslike movement through the tousled curls.

Amanda's smooth brow furled with consternation. "Lucas, what's the matter? What's happened?" Her hands seized his jacket sleeves. "Are your folks all right?"

He captured her fingers, threading them between his own. "Nothing is the matter, and my folks are just fine. My mother is still raving over that peignoir set you sent her for Christmas."

Tilting her head, Amanda aimed an accusing glance. "Then what are you doing here?"

"You make it sound like I've flown in from another planet instead of Dallas," Lucas teased. His knuckles landed a velvet punch against her jaw. "On the expert advice of my tax man, I've decided to contribute some hard-earned bucks to the Cancer Society. I packed my black tie and came to view your latest triumph." His arm made a gallant sweep toward the stage.

"Lucas, I don't believe you for a minute," came her peremptory announcement. "Your right eyebrow always wiggles when you lie." Amanda folded her arms across her breasts; the toe of her shoe tapped a censuring refrain against the gold-and-green patterned carpet.

"It's a damn good thing you'll never sit in one of my juries," he grumbled, eyes half-hooded from her ominous gaze. Lucas winced and rubbed his face. "All right, Mandy, if you want to know the truth, I was damn worried about you."

"Why?"

"Why?" He gave an exasperated snort. "Because when I called last week and sang 'Happy Birthday,' my off-key baritone didn't get its usual laugh." It was his turn to focus an interrogative stare. "I didn't even get a conciliatory chuckle, just a polite thank you for the earrings." He sucked in his cheeks. "*Too* polite."

"Lucas, I love the earrings." Her thumb and forefinger caressed the gold leafs that dangled from her lobe. "You mean you came here just because I didn't sound right?"

"Call it ESP. I remember flying much farther on the same feeling."

Amanda found herself blinking rapidly, anxious to disperse the dampness that stung her eyes. "Look, your psychic radar is off. You just caught me on a bad day," she chided, forcing a smile. "Turning thirty is a big milestone. I guess I was lonely and still suffering jet lag from the Paris buying trip and working on this show and—"

"Mandy," Lucas interrupted, lifting her chin to study artfully controlled features, "I can always tell when you're lying. A rain cloud forms over those crystal irises."

"And how could you tell that through the telephone lines?"

He grinned, the indentations clefting his cheeks. "I don't need to see you. I can tell more by what you *don't* say. I know you better than your mother. Whom I called, by the way."

"Lucas!" She stamped her foot and turned her back.

"Mandy," his deep voice curled into her inner ear, his warm breath made the leaf shiver, "come on. Tell me what's really bothering you. Your letters and phone calls have only given me the surface." His hands slid up her arms, curved around her shoulders to pull her against him. "I think it's time we had one of our meaningful dialogues."

17

A chuckle escaped her. *Meaningful dialogue.* She had started using that phrase when they were in college. It was true then and now. She and Lucas had always been able to talk, to communicate, to exchange ideas and even to fight without ever jeopardizing their relationship. They had achieved intellectual parity. Their friendship enriched one another's life. They related to each other as people. What they had was very rare, very exquisite—a mutual caring that had stood time and distance, growing ever stronger and richer over the years.

"Lucas, I am glad you're here," Amanda finally admitted. Her smooth cheek rubbed against his. The masculine stubble and the warm, spicy scent of Cardin proved an instant balm. "If I were to tell you what's been on my mind lately, you'd have arrived with a straitjacket."

"Never! As I recall you look ghastly in white, and those back closures are definitely last year—very gauche. Why, my dear—"

Her laughter interrupted his effeminate, nasal affectation. "How long can you stay?"

"I'm booked on the noon plane on Sunday." Lucas rested his chin on her shoulder. The butter-soft suede nuzzled his skin. "Come on, stop hedging." A pair of well-muscled arms wrapped around Amanda like the aforementioned straitjacket. "What's the problem?"

"That is the problem. My days are wine and roses and I'm wishing for thorns." At his insistent squeeze, she sighed and became more specific. "Most women hit thirty and try to 'find themselves,' always searching," Amanda continued after a moment's hesitation. "I've known what I wanted since I was sixteen. I followed the direct course and now"—her lips twisted into a rueful smile—"now I've got it, got it all."

"Aren't you happy?"

"Yes, Lucas, I am happy." She took a deep, reflective breath. "I own my own business, which despite the economy is doing so well it scares me. I have an excellent manager, the sales staff all love their jobs, the customers are faithful and my ego wallows in all the local publicity."

"I'm hearing a but."

She shrugged, wincing when she pumped his chin. "B-u-t. Three little letters that mean so much more." Amanda pulled free of his embrace. "It was turning the big three-oh. I grew up early. Maybe that's why I feel so over-the-hill."

Lucas sat back in the gold upholstered dining chair. "If you feel middle-aged, what about me? I've got five years on you."

"But your career commitment is growing stronger." She pulled out the chair next to him, her palms flat against his knees. "You've just embarked on another challenge, opening your own law practice. Don't tell me that a heady mixture of fear and excitement isn't flowing through your veins! That's the best high—an unbelievable high."

He gave her a wide smile. "You hit that right. Fear and excitement are a most provocative pair."

Amanda exhaled a sigh. "That's my problem. Lack of provocation." She raised a defensive palm. "Don't say it. I know I'm acting like a selfish, spoiled only child. I should be happy and content with what I have. And it makes me angry that I'm not." She leaned against the chair, exhaustion and relief making her groggy. "I'm already at my peak. I've accomplished my goals. What else is there?"

"What about the fashion shows?"

Her hand pushed away the thought. "They were a challenge at first, but . . ." Her voice drifted off.

"Burnout."

Amanda shook her head. "Boredom," she corrected. "I'm like a hamster on a treadmill. Running, running, but only my body gets exercised—not my mind, not my creativity, not my talent."

"When was the last time you had a vacation?"

"I just got back from Paris."

He gave her a knowing look. "Since when is a buying trip a vacation?"

"Actually it's a transformation," she returned with a grimace. "You're reshaped into a very delicious, very expensive bonbon. Served at all the parties, wedged into the

19

showings, sprinkled with sugary gifts." Her eyes closed.
"You're right, it's no vacation. You're always on guard,
trying to get the jump on another buyer. Fashion retail is a
glamorous profession, one that gives moments of vitality,
but lately it's just a job."

One gray eye opened and peered at him. "If I tell you another secret, will you promise not to laugh?" At Lucas' affirmative nod, Amanda reclosed her eyes. "For the past
twelve years my main commitment has been to my job. It's
been my first love. But lately," her voice grew slightly
melancholy, "I feel the urge to settle down. The old nesting
instinct. I want to have the two point five children, the sta-
tion wagon and the flea-ridden dog."

"Does this have anything to do with Brian Neuman?"

"Brian?" Her eyelids opened, astonished that he would
remember a name he'd heard just once. "Brian and I were
in 'heavy like' but . . ." She sighed again. "You explain it
to me, Lucas. Why is it when two people are nice, eligible
and bright, the pieces just don't fit. Not for happily ever after."

"I don't know, Mandy." Lucas took possession of her
right hand. "I've often asked myself that same question."
He traced her slender wrist, then each elegant polished
fingernail. "It never seems to be a physical incompatibil-
ity, just the intangibles. That's what makes a relationship
all or nothing."

"Isn't that the case. You want the one thing you can't
put your finger on." Amanda cleared her throat, her
smoky gaze focusing on their intimate coupling of hands.
"Are you still seeing Kitty Byrnes?"

"We just celebrated six weeks."

"That sounds promising."

Lucas gave a diffident shrug. "Sometimes I think so,
then again . . ." His voice drifted off. "We seem to have to
work awfully hard at it. A relationship shouldn't be like
that." Hazel eyes regarded her. "You and I never had that
trouble."

"Lucas," she chastised, "we were never after anything
physical. We're Plato's ideal—nonsexual lovers." Amanda

balanced her left elbow on her knee and set her chin in her palm. "But now you know what I'm going through both personally and professionally. So positive one minute, so confused the next. It's a merry-go-round I'd like to get off."

A pair of masculine hands gently patted her cheeks, bringing a soft flush to her pale complexion. "That's why I'm here, kid. I've got a proposition for you."

"Proposition?" she returned archly. "As I recall you once accused me of not knowing the difference between a proposition and a preposition!"

"Listen, any girl who would go out with a guy nick-named 'Cherry Picker' deserved to be ridiculed."

"Charlie was a perfect gentleman."

"Don't sound so damn disappointed." Lucas gave her his most charming smile. "My proposition is on the up and up."

Amanda's lips twisted. "Hmmm." Her suspicions grew as his smile broadened, even white teeth giving a wolfish grin. "Come on, Lucas, give. What is—" The footlights began to flicker, a sinuous electric glow arched and twisted to the rhythmic taped piano intro.

She let out a groan. "Look what you've done, Lucas Crosse! I've forgotten all about the show!" Her gaze swung to the wall clock. "Damn! Look at the time."

Grabbing his hand, she yanked Lucas' six-foot frame off the chair. "Come on, boy, I've got a proposition for you. Just stand at the end of the runway and let the models get a look at that handsome face. The sight of a man like you should put some fire into their steps."

Lucas contemplated a willowy redhead in a snowy silk Charmeuse gown. "I think I'm the one on fire," his deep voice rumbled in Amanda's ear. He zeroed in on Lizette's entrance. The narrow gold halter and sheer metallic-veined harem pants she was wearing sent an erotic message of delights in a sordid sand epic. "Is there a theme to this lascivious madness?"

" 'A Taste of Elegance.' " Amanda balanced an elbow on his shoulder; her two-inch heels put them on equal footing.

"The fashions are as piquant and varied as tonight's Creole cuisine."

Lucas' hazel eyes widened to scrutinize every sassy inch of the red Lurex and black lace teddy that wriggled toward him. "You mean I'm getting more than chicken à la king?"

"Perish the thought." A gentle elbow registered her objection to his statement. "Chef Jean-Claude is preparing the favorite specialties of our leading restaurants while I serve more visual fare.

"Swimsuits and sportswear accompany the chicken and okra gumbo; daytime and evening fashions help you digest red snapper and oyster and shrimp jambalaya, and these confections will put an extra dollop of *crème* on the *brûlée.*" Amanda smiled at his hypnotized countenance. "What do you think? *Très* chic?"

A powder-pink, diagonally puffed teddy displayed an ample portion of Felicia's rounded *derrière.* "*Très* cheeky," Lucas concluded, eyebrows raising in salute.

"A little too . . ." Amanda made a mental note to have Bianca adjust another of Felicia's garments.

"Is that Duke Ellington I hear?"

"Hmm, I was a little hesitant about using tapes, but it makes the blending easier, and the engineering student who's been helping out matched the music to the lights. We're having a dance band after dinner."

"The food, the fashions and the music are sure to excite even the most finicky." Lucas slid an arm around her shoulders. "If the appetizers and entrées look like the dessert, you'll have a gastronomical delight on your hands."

"Thank you, kind sir." Amanda turned her attention to Isaac Bevans. "It looked and sounded just perfect." She complimented with a smile. "Why don't you head for home and take a break. We've got ninety minutes before show time." Then she added, "Please tell Bianca and Felicia I'd like to see them."

"Lucas," she whispered as her black lashes fluttered like lace butterflies, "when are you going to tell me about this proposition?"

He smiled at her mock-coquettishness and shook his

head. "I'm allying myself with your production ideas and letting you stew." Lucas pushed his tongue against his cheek, laughing when her tongue wagged at him.

"Come on, please," she cajoled in her best little-girl voice, fingers walking a few provocative steps along his lapels. "I could be really nasty and stop sending you these nice designer samples."

"Feminine wiles will not work on me, Amanda." He slapped her hands playfully. "I could be really nasty and start billing you for legal services." His lips curved upward despite his brusque declaration. "I'll tell you all about it tonight while we celebrate your triumph."

She exhaled in frustration. "All right, be mysterious." Her pert nose wrinkled in disgust. "Do you remember how to get to my duplex?" Amanda reached into her skirt pocket, then tossed him a set of house keys.

"Who could forget the beautiful view of Lake Pontchartrain?" Lucas nodded toward the two women walking onstage. "I'm going to let you get back to work. I'll see you tonight." Lifting her chin, he planted a light kiss on her slightly shining nose.

With an exasperated sigh at Lucas' departing figure, Amanda went back to work. "The finale went very well, Bianca. Did you have any problems?"

Mme. Dupree nodded toward the gum-chewing model. "Only with this little one," she returned on a high sarcastic note.

Felicia pursed her lips, and the gum formed a large pink bubble. She back-popped it and grinned at Amanda. "It was all the goodies from Easter." Her brown eyes slanted toward the ballroom. "Who was that? He's cute."

"I'll tell him you said that." Amanda untied the pink, coral and beige bow that circled her waist. "Can this be lowered a bit in the back?"

Bianca shrugged. Her blue gaze was more interested in assessing Amanda's glowing features than the fit of the powder-puffed teddy. "You are looking much better since he arrived. That man, he is special, yes?"

"Very." She held her breath for the upcoming barrage.

"Your lover, yes?" Bianca pulled at the nylon mitered lace at Felicia's hips.

"No." Amanda turned the model around, pointedly ignoring Felicia's giggles. *"Amite en rose,"* she explained to the gray-haired *couturière*. "We have a very special, very old friendship."

"I'd want more than friendship." The model popped another bubble. "Unless," she twisted her neck around. "He's gay, right?"

"No."

"Then he can't get it on with a woman?"

"No!" Amanda gave an exasperated snort. "Honestly, Felicia, don't you have any men who are just friends?"

"Uh-uh." The pink gum made a series of popping noises. "It's against nature. You two have to be having an affair."

"An affair of the heart," agreed Bianca, favoring Amanda with a knowing wink. "He is good for you. It shows already."

"Lucas is like the brother I never had," Amanda repeated with unnecessary force. "There is nothing romantic between us."

"Brother, huh." Felicia pushed at the sensuous blond curls that haphazardly tumbled around her neck. "If I were you, I'd think about incest."

"If I were you," Amanda returned in a cool voice, her fingers pressing against a mound of cellulite, "I'd think about Weight Watchers."

Chapter Two

THE CHICKEN AND OKRA gumbo was rich, succulent and hot; the wailing trumpet backed by saxophone and piano was fluid, smooth and cool. As the houselights dimmed, blanketing the ballroom in candle-flickering darkness, Lucas Crosse and the three hundred other dinner patrons savored spoonfuls of the pungent, condiment-laden soup.

A crimson-edged spotlight centered against the voluptuous emerald stage curtains and focused on what Lucas could only blinkingly classify a "vision." Ornate Reed & Barton silver clattered against chaste Mikasa bowls. Appetites were piqued, but eyes had turned more greedy than stomach.

Cayenne and red pepper had stimulated palates, but Amanda Wyatt enthralled the diners even more than the Creole *haute cuisine*. Sharp and exciting to the mind and senses was this tall, lithe, wholly feminine addition to the menu.

Amanda floated down the lengthy runway with provocative buoyancy. Her well-modulated voice caressed ears via a hand-held wireless microphone as she welcomed one and all to the Cancer Society's spring gala: "A Taste of Elegance."

Elegance. Lucas shook his head, his dark gaze riveted on Amanda. What an inadequate word. Panache. Class. Charm. Magic. The thesaurus would fail in its duties at this moment. Like the definition of Creole, Amanda Wyatt reflected the spice, the delicacy and the skill native to New Orleans.

25

Along with three hundred other entranced listeners, Lucas followed her honeyed words of instruction and directed his attention to the celebration of a splendid figure swathed in a Givenchy creation. The dramatic lipstick-red silk sheath snaked around womanly accouterments, swirled to the floor and set hearts palpitating with its high voltage.

The extravagant jacquard *fourreau* was an exciting lure suspended from supple shoulders by thin straps. Clinging to and defining Amanda's full bosom—an impertinent black silk rose accentuating the seductive cleavage—the material wrapped slim hips, then ruffled in a bustlelike pouf against a rounded *derrière*.

Lucas and the other guests were informed that the gown had been created for Audrey Hepburn by Hubert de Givenchy in the fifties. Somehow Lucas felt the accomplished actress could hardly have done this masterpiece as much justice as its present occupant.

Amanda's makeup and decidedly outrageous manner complemented the wicked nighttime glamor created by the French couture and paraphrased the spice-rich appetizer. Kohl shadow added intrigue to those quartz irises that flashed bolts of coquettish enticement toward the captivated house. Her scarlet-tinted lips transformed innocent words into *double-entendres* that teased and titillated rather than offended. The chestnut curls that haloed in a precise flourish managed to generate the impression that she had just tumbled off a pillow after a sensual coupling.

Despite the formal elegance of her gown, there was nothing tame about Amanda's performance. Lucas observed the effect it had on his nine tablemates. The women responded not with catty, jealous remarks but with admiration-tinged envy. He didn't doubt each one was fantasizing she was on that stage, commanding attention and impromptu applause.

The men, despite their age and sartorial, tuxedoed splendor, seemed overwhelmed by a case of locker-room adolescent puberty. Lucas found he was no exception. The saucy, sassy, seductive lady in red struck a libidinous chord in every man in the room.

Perhaps it was the way Amanda's long fingers caressed and stroked the microphone and the close proximity of her vivid mouth to its bulbous head. The phallic-symboled electronic amplifier conjured a most provocative image. Hormones collided. Primitive biological urges made inertia quite painful. His own emotions in a state of bedevilment, Lucas hastily tried to divert himself by redirecting his attention to the hearty provincial soup that was studded with tender chicken cubes and succulent oysters. But the savory composition was only a momentary diversion from his thoughts of Amanda.

A few hours ago, Lucas had marveled at the physical changes two years had made. Now he discovered a more complex individual, who left him even more astounded and confused. From where had this Amanda Wyatt sprung?

Lucas had thought he was familiar with every facet of her personality. But this was an Amanda he had yet to discover. Again, the stage attracted his attention. His eyes stalked the laughing, beguiling female strutting on the runway. This image didn't jibe with his memories in which Amanda shared the same status as his two younger sisters.

This teasing provocation was erotic and sensual. Lucas could feel himself responding to her earthiness in a resonant overture of his own. Shifting uncomfortably against the padded dining seat, he chided himself for the purely sexual reaction. Hadn't he exhausted himself last night with Kitty Byrnes?

That's it, Lucas thought as he toyed with his array of silverware, *concentrate on Kitty.* In the six weeks he had known her their rapid acceleration into physical intimacy had surprised him, but Kitty was a self-proclaimed "new woman." Giddy over her monetarily surging career and bursting with the most liberated outward behavior, her unabashed sexuality was a personal declaration of independence.

A reminiscent smile curved Lucas' lips. Kitty was an exceptional lover—active, inventive, uninhibited and totally committed to mutual nirvana. Last night, having negotiated a six-figure real-estate transaction, she had been on a natural high and he had reaped the rewards.

It had been an evening with Pol Roger bubbling in tulipshaped Fostoria, Black Diamond steaks and total relaxation, courtesy of a Jacuzzi built for two. They had massaged each other with fragrant oil and shared the sunlamp that gave Kitty's petite anatomy a St. Tropez tan twelve months a year. When inner heat threatened to short-circuit the infrared lamp, they gravitated to her canopied four-poster.

Lucas' thumb and forefinger smoothed the gold linen napkin that protected his evening jacket. The lustrous flaxen material duplicated Kitty's soft, pale straw-colored sweep of hair. The sensitive skin on his inner thigh tingled against the remembered teasing silkiness of her saunadampened tresses.

Twitching with embarrassed discomfort, Lucas hurriedly forfeited the rest of the spicy gumbo. "Damn oysters" came his muttered oath. Had this bewitching Amanda arranged that aphrodisiac oysters be part of the menu? His hazel eyes diligently searched for some nonerotic focal point.

His gaze turned skyward to the white-lace gazebo that cocooned his table. But the latticework only reminded him of the folksy shawllike canopy over Kitty's Queen Anne bed. Lucas found his carbonated blood racing like quicksilver and his body hardening against an invisible mouth, tongue and hands that coaxed and urged.

But it wasn't Kitty Byrnes' sapphire eyes and delicate, patrician face that swam into focus. The eyes that seared Lucas' brain were almond-shaped and as mysterious as fog; the face fuller, with lips infinitely more inviting.

Nor did he imagine Kitty's small, firm breasts against the dark, curly hair of his thighs, moving to titillate his flat stomach and chest all the while working ever closer to his anxious mouth. The sleekly graceful feline that stealthily consumed his naked length with her own was Amanda. It was she who possessed his engorged spirit, enmeshing it with the core of her femininity and absorbing the very essence of his desire.

"Excuse me, sir." The waiter's low whisper made Lucas jump. The steward was quick, easily maneuvering the half-full soup bowl from the suddenly hazardous environment.

Lucas gulped a self-conscious mouthful of cold water; his tongue procured a small ice cube that he hoped would send continued waves of common sense through his system. Chastising himself for his thoughts, he concentrated on the "old" Amanda. His buddy, his pal. That fiercely independent girl who needed free reign.

Their relationship has been one of growth and injury and repair and mutual aid. It had always been an intimate friendship, but the intimacy was one of the mind, not the flesh. Why then were his thoughts drifting toward the latter? Lucas picked up his fork, twisting the silver to catch the candlelight; if he didn't put his own feelings in proper perspective his initial plan of action would be lost. Suddenly he wanted to win with a vengeance.

The salad vinaigrette proved tart and crisp—the perfect remedy for the aphrodisiacal appetizer. Amanda had retired to safety behind the speaker's podium and was introducing the first collection. Sportswear-clad models whirled and twisted to the dulcet tones of Dave Brubeck.

Between bits of fresh spinach and crunchy vegetables, Lucas viewed the stylish parade with haunted eyes. Eating, drinking and applauding became rote. The ballroom, the people, the music drifted into hazy oblivion, replaced with a twelve-year-old memory that took on three-dimensional clarity.

Women were still on parade but they had teenage faces, their long, straight hair was parted in the middle and pressed against acne-spattered cheeks. Baggy shirts and jeans that wouldn't bend emphasized a wide range of body shapes—some Twiggy-thin, others harboring high-school baby fat.

"Who'd UNIVAC pick for you, Crosse?" Ben Collins' deep baritone rang alive in his ear.

"A. J. Wyatt from Greensboro, North Carolina." Lucas' voice was pure magnolia and mint julep; his southern accent got the intended laugh. "What the hell, maybe this good ole boy will fill the vacancy on the freshman basketball team."

Ben's lanky frame pressed against the concrete auditorium wall; he shook his head at the antlike crowd of confused freshman arrivals. "I don't think Herschel Wyland sounds like the sports type," he said and sighed, folding his green-and-white computer printout into an airplane. The paper craft made a perfect loop before crash-landing against his sneaker.

They spent the next few minutes dissecting and rating the new coeds when Herschel stumbled toward them. He was just what Ben had predicted—a timid, squeaky-voiced youth from the farm belt who viewed his first year at New York University with wide-eyed wonder. Lucas helped Ben to calm and orient his freshman "buddy." The senior program was designed to prevent new arrivals from getting lost among the thirty thousand students who inhabited the sprawling campus.

"One of you named Crosse?"

The unmistakable female voice that interrupted meant the basketball coach was down one player, although the leggy, coltish figure that focused stormy eyes on a level with Lucas' own would have done the team some good.

"Wyatt, A. J.—Amanda," the first name was reluctantly offered, as was the yellow registration punch card. "I didn't expect a babysitter. How long?"

Lucas resisted the impulse to yank the copper-brown braid that hung over one shoulder. "The whole year." His vexed gaze shifted to Ben's grinning face. Herschel was going to be a piece of cake compared to his *buddy*. "Just think of me as a replacement for your brother."

"I'm an only child."

It figures! Lucas gave an inward grimace and watched Amanda tumble a blue knapsack off her back.

She pulled a perspiration-soaked madras shirt free of her khaki slacks. "Aren't you a little old to still be on campus?" Amanda said as she pointedly assessed his face, making him shift in discomfort.

He didn't like her superior attitude. It made *him* feel like the freshman. "Uncle Sam borrowed me for two years." Lucas locked his thumbs into the empty belt loops on his denim cutoffs. "Want to see my shrapnel scars?" He waited for her face to burn.

"Why don't we save the show-and-tell for a rainy day," she returned, totally nonplussed. "I've had a long, hot bus trip and I want to see my dorm."

When he reached for her rucksack, Lucas found that a feminine hand had already claimed the padded strap. "Don't tell me you're one of those butch bra-burners?" he snapped, as his anger was rapidly depleting his patience.

Amanda blinked, then laughed, even, white teeth more pronounced against a late-summer, biscuit-tanned complexion. When she spoke her tone had softened. "It took me too long to fill a B cup." She paused, then stepped to one side. "I'm leaving the heavy stuff for you, buddy." His muffled grunt at the size of her red steamer trunk elicited another chuckle.

The trunk was heaved over broad shoulders, and Lucas led the way across Washington Square Park to the designated dorm. "You are not the usual twittering, uncertain freshman."

"I'm an Army brat."

"That says it all, kid," he said dryly, but in his mind he exhaled a pent-up breath. Amanda Wyatt was calm, cool and unflappable—better tough than sniveling.

"I've seen latrines with more promise than this." She shook her head at the single room with its fresh coat of putty-colored paint. "Well, I've only got two years to live in this cell." Plunking herself on the padded window seat, Amanda stared at the tiny room.

"Two years?" Lucas dropped the trunk on the narrow, unmade cot. "What's your major?"

"You're looking at the next Chanel or Schiaparelli," returned a proud voice.

"Music?"

A disgusted groan assaulted his ears. Amanda stalked across the room, grabbed his shoulders and peered into his eyes. "Are you on a maryjane cloud?"

Lucas freed one eyelid from her fingertips. "I don't drink more than two beers on the weekend but I'm beginning to wonder about you."

"I still chew baby aspirin." She exhaled a forbearing breath. "I'm a fashion designer."

"You should have gone directly to the Parsons School of Design or the Fashion Institute of Technology," Lucas pointed out with succinct authority.

Amanda shoved the trunk onto the gray-and-beige carpet, replacing its position on the blue-ticked mattress with herself. "Sit down, Lucas." She patted a seat for him. "Since we're going to be Siamese twins, I might as well regale you with my eight-year life plan."

"Only eight!" He hadn't tried to hide the mocking grin that split his features.

"To get to New York City," she blithely continued, "I had to pacify my parents and agree to a two-year program at NYU. But I really don't mind. I can add some business courses to my art, and then I'll enroll in FIT. I'll be there two years and then," Amanda paused, licking her lips and savoring the next word, "Paris. After that, I'll be the toast of Seventh Avenue, and one day I'll own my own boutique, designing for a chosen few."

"I think a crash course in humility might come in handy," Lucas countered, shaking his head at her sublime expression.

"Why should I be humble?" she said breezily as she leaned over, snapped the trunk latches and lifted out a sketch pad. "Feast your eyes, Crosse." Her long fingers reverently turned page after page, inviting his inspection. "When I was fifteen I created Barbie clothes that would have made Dior green with envy."

He shrugged in bewilderment. "I'm studying law, not art or fashion or—"

"And I'm stuck with you for a whole year!" She slammed the heavy cardboard cover closed, caught the tip of his nose and didn't utter one word of apology.

"The feeling is mutual, Wyatt." Lucas massaged the sting from his nostrils, watching as she emptied the steamer. Clothes were hung in the small wardrobe in a precise pattern, others neatly folded in the built-in bureau.

Grudgingly, he had to admit Amanda Wyatt had it all together. Eighteen and positive. She had defined her target and zeroed in. As a freshman, he had waffled over his major, letting his first year go liberal arts; he had decided on law in a rice paddy in 'Nam. "I'll come and take you to breakfast tomorrow and then we'll attend the orientation meeting."

As Amanda's head turned, the thick braid slapped her right breast. "You eat breakfast for me, Crosse, and if they call my name at the meeting, tell them I'm in the infirmary with ptomaine."

"What?"

"I'm headed for the garment district and a job." Her hands settled on slim hips and her eyes narrowed in defiance. "What did you think this was, a free ride? My folks aren't paying my way. I got a partial scholarship in art and spent the past three summers smiling my way through half a million cheeseburgers. I need to make some bucks while I'm here."

"Listen, *brat*," Lucas towered as best he could over her formidable height, "you'd better be ready at 7:00 A.M. sharp or you'll have to design something to cover a black-and-blue butt!"

Amanda had stood him up for both breakfast and the meeting. He remembered pacing a hole through the rubber soles of his tennis shoes. When she finally returned, she was grinning from ear to ear. He was grinning too, but it was a satanical one, motivated by thoughts of homicide and a strong defense built around temporary insanity.

"You really take the proverbial cake," he'd rallied. One

large hand closed around her wrist, pulling her through the doorway and propelling her sideways to the neatly made up cot. "One day, twenty-four stinking hours on campus and you think you're in command. I have never met . . . you are the most . . . I . . ." his anger made coherent vocalization impossible.

Amanda straightened out her brown sundress, then let her thumbs and hands form a U-shaped window. "I bet you're a perfect specimen."

"What?"

"A forty regular," her chestnut braid switched shoulders, "size fifteen shirt?" Amanda opened the blue plastic bag suspended from her wrist and pulled out an oxford cloth dress shirt. "This is courtesy of Seymour the Haberdasher."

"What?"

She shook her head and tossed him the shirt. "Crosse, you're beginning to sound like a parrot. I thought lawyers were articulate."

"I am very articulate when I'm dealing with a sane person!" Lucas took a deep breath, counted to ten but didn't get a chance to say one word.

"I'll be working at Seymour's Shirts four hours a day and till noon on Saturday as a go-fer." Amanda's voice dropped to a conspiratorial whisper. "I'm getting sixty bucks under the table plus the pick of the seconds for you." A sparkling gray eye favored him with a wink. "Seymour's cousin designs sportswear for tall women, and every other Friday I'll be modeling for late-night buyers. I'm a perfect size eight."

"You're too skinny." To this day Lucas still wondered why he had ever said that!

Amanda laughed, leaned back against the wall, a pillow snuggled against her breasts. "What a day! Lucas, it was fantastic! Seventh Avenue is like . . . like a beehive gone berserk."

She kicked off her sandals and arranged herself full length on the sunset-colored India-print bedspread. "I walked through eighteen blocks filled with dress racks, trucks and handcarts. I went through picture-perfect showrooms into workrooms of unpainted steel, overhead pipes and a million humming sewing machines.

"Everyone was yelling and screaming and eating. Phones never stopped ringing. At lunchtime the streets were strangled with people." Amanda exhaled a genuine sigh of pleasure. "It was congested, hurried and high-strung." She smothered a yawn. "It was wonderful."

Lucas stared down at her. His anger ebbed into oblivion. The glow on her face was more eloquent than words. Amanda had turned the drudgery of everyday into something magic and lyrical. He found her enthusiasm contagious. Pushing her long legs to one side, Lucas had sat on the narrow mattress and demanded a minute-by-minute replay of her day, anxious to embrace her fever as his own.

By the end of Amanda's first month at NYU and Seymour's, Lucas had three new shirts and a new sweater vest hanging in his closet. He was also taking a lot of heat from his friends. "Score yet with Wyatt?" became the byword of his dorm, but Lucas had refused to let the locker-room mentality of his cronies put an end to a friendship that had become almost vital to him.

Amanda had given him a validation of his own worth and something more: courage. Not the courage he had discovered fighting in Southeast Asia, but the courage to ignore peer-group pressure and listen to his inner conscience. She proved the perfect panacea to his cynicism; the elixer needed to perk up the tedium that invaded his studies. Lucas found he embraced each day with a passion; his improved grades reiterated that assertion.

It was mid-October before Amanda's initial bravado wore off. College proved more of everything than high school, and her added work schedule didn't help. A child emerged. She became hesitant, homesick, and confused. He had been there to make the transition easier. Since he had gone through experiences similar to hers, his support gave her confidence.

His advice was impartial, not parental. He wasn't there to protect or censor. In talking to him, Amanda was able to discover the answers to her own questions. They fed off each other's stability, fears, loneliness and humor—with no strings attached.

"You are proving to be the big brother I never realized I missed having," Amanda had said, sniffing against his collar one cold, sleeting December afternoon. She had been desolated about not being asked to a freshman holiday mixer. "I couldn't have dropped more hints to Randy if I had encased them in concrete. Why do all you tall guys prefer to date the most petite girls? It's just not fair."

"Randall Henderson is a dumb jock." Lucas hunted through his pockets for a handkerchief. She took it even though it was smeared with grease from the oil dipstick on his car. "Consider yourself lucky, kid. Would you really want to spend a perfectly good Saturday night gagging on fruit punch and stale cookies?"

"Yes." She had said it so positively they both had laughed. Her low voice droned into his ear, her chin settled into a comfortable niche on his shoulder. "My mother asked me that same question about my junior prom and senior ball. I didn't get asked to them either."

"Were there any guys with brains in your high school?"

"Brains, yes. Height, no. I was taller than the center on the basketball team. I was also gawky, skinny, awkward and pimpled."

Lucas had wiped an oil streak from her smooth cheek and made appropriate clucking noises. "Now you are a model."

Amanda brightened considerably. "You always say the perfect thing, Crosse. I envy your sisters." Her eyelids closed, her lips formed a smirk that made him shift uneasily. "Want to know a secret, Lucas?"

"Oh-oh."

"When I was twelve, I was taller than all the boys and all the girls in my class. They picked on me and laughed at me. I was very lonely, and moving from Army base to Army base didn't help." Her voice had a little-girl singsong quality. "I'd come home from school, curl up securely on my bed and draw the ugliest clothes I could think of for those tiny, doll-like girls to wear. I'd make believe they had no choice but to buy the horrible designs I created, and then everyone would point and laugh at them."

"You were a brat."

"It was therapy."

"How about some Lucas Crosse therapy? We can gorge on pepperoni pizza and see the Bogart Film Festival."

"Sounds infinitely better than sour punch and dry cookies, and you are decidedly better than Randall Henderson."

Decidedly better than Randall Henderson. Lucas pushed aside the plate that held the remains of a mild, subtle red snapper. Why was it, even twelve years later, he could still remember the name of Amanda's first college crush? Maybe because there were so few names to recall.

Amanda had been all work and no play, at times morbidly self-conscious about her height and lack of suitors. He had been there to massage her bruised ego, to make her laugh. "It's nice to have you give the *older* male viewpoint, Crosse."

She had been there to impart the female point of view. She had never been impressed with his "big man on campus" status, and he had been frankly relieved. With Amanda, Lucas found he never had to project a false image. He never thought of her as a coed. She was a buddy—a neuter.

Lucas' gaze became centered on the woman behind the speaker's lectern. Amanda was no longer gawky or skinny. She was the best friend he would ever have. Still a buddy, but definitely not a neuter. She was strong, healthy, competent and self-assured. The ultimate woman.

Again the richness of his feelings began to rouse that subtle sexual tension he had experienced earlier. Lucas relocated his emotions to Kitty. Her initial brashness had reminded him of Amanda. Kitty was young, eager and positive but much more a social creature than Amanda had ever been. Kitty focused on the superficial; she was not yet mature enough to drop her social mask. Amanda had been knowledgeable enough to realize how little flashy externals counted.

While the audience was absorbed in the slide presentation and speech by the director of the Cancer Society, Lucas once again retreated to an inner world. He tried to recall how their lives had become so entwined. Most of the seniors had gradually abandoned their freshman buddies, but his friendship with Amanda had grown and solidified. He had met her family during their first spring break.

"What do you mean, you're not going anywhere?" She'd frowned, stuffing another bathing suit into her knapsack.

"Just that. I'm tapped. Busted. Broke. I ran into a few expenses that I hadn't planned on."

"You mean you ran into Sandra Perry, the campus barracuda." It was said with an I-told-you-so smugness that made him blush. "Go back to your dorm and pack, Crosse. We'll cash in my plane ticket and take the bus."

"Are you serious?"

"North Carolina is green in March, Lucas, and bathed in sunshine." Amanda gestured toward her frost-edged window. "New York still has snow, naked trees and gray skies." She grinned at him. "Room and board are free. My dad will love adopting you for two weeks. He'll teach you golf. All lawyers should play golf. Do you know how many cases are settled on golf courses?"

He had been uncomfortable about meeting her parents. "How are you going to explain me?"

Amanda stopped sketching and looked at him. "Is that the reason you've been wriggling in this bus seat for the past ten hours?" She laughed. "My parents know all about you, Lucas. They think you've been a healthy influence on me." Her voice toughened. "If you dare squeal about my working at Seymour's, I'll cut off your supply of free shirts."

His jaw dropped. "You mean they don't know about your job?" She gave him a Cheshire-cat grin. "Where did you tell them you were getting your money?"

"From working at the campus bookstore." Amanda

interrupted his strangled rebuttal with: "By the way, Crosse, even though my dad retired from the Army last month, he still expects to be saluted twice a day."

Brigadier General (Ret.) William Wyatt may have commanded troops during World War II and Korea, but it was evident he had little say in the operation of his own home. Amanda's tall, slim mother, Anne, ruled the sprawling white ranch house, filling it with little formality but lots of food, laughter and easy conversation.

Lucas instantly felt at home. The general did teach him the rudiments of golf, but they both preferred fishing in Salem Lake. Between swilling cans of beer and hooking white perch, they swapped Army stories and Amanda stories. "That daughter of mine is as independent as they come. If she had ever enlisted she would have only seen the stockade." Clouds of fragrant pipe smoke emphasized each word. "I bet she's given you more headaches and indigestion than you thought possible."

Lucas could still feel the splinters from the weathered boat seat stab through his clothes. "Amanda certainly has kept me from being bored, sir." It was still true—you could accuse Amanda Wyatt of many things, but she was never boring.

North Carolina and the Wyatts' became his home during the next three spring breaks. Later, Lucas enjoyed their hospitality during his vacations from the district attorney's office. Amanda's introduction to the Crosse clan came at the end of her first year.

"When are you heading home?" Lucas had inquired while they were soaping up the side of his blue Mustang.

"Don't yell," Amanda forewarned, bending to scour what were supposed to be whitewalls. "I've taken my dorm room for the summer. Seymour's cousin—"

"Another cousin?"

"Seymour is smothered with cousins," she said grinning. "Anyway, I've signed on to cut patterns. It's great experience. I talked to my folks—and I mean *talked*—but they finally agreed. When you come back for law school, you'll have a couple of winter suits and I'll have a rejuvenated bank balance and lots of firsthand knowledge."

He threw the sponge in the direction of the soap-filled bucket. "Let me guess: This is all under the table, and I bet it's sweatshop conditions."

"I'm counting on you to have your law degree and defend me by the time the IRS catches on."

"I don't like it."

Amanda stood up and glared at him. Her icy-gray gaze defied the authority in his voice. "You don't have to like it, Crosse. I start in two weeks."

"Then you'll spend the next fourteen days in Maine with me," he told her rudely. "At least you'll get some type of vacation."

"There's still snow in Maine."

"Very funny. I've got a job working on bridge construction with my father's company. I'm sure my mother and sisters would be delighted to have your sweet personality grace their home." He gave a warning yank on her braid. "I expect you to be on your best behavior. A little humble, a little meek, a little ingratiating and no steamroller tactics."

Amanda picked up the green garden hose, aiming it toward the soap-covered fender. "Don't you think I can be all those things, Lucas?" He had made the mistake of shaking his head. "You're absolutely right!" She turned on the nozzle, swung the hose and caught him full in the face and chest.

Amanda had spoken the truth. She was never anything but herself, yet his family was immediately captivated. His mother, Vera, took him aside, telling him she wished his sisters, Kathy and Margaret, respectively a year younger and two years older than Amanda, would duplicate her maturity and capabilities.

His sisters became Amanda's pen pals, trading letters full of girl talk and college woes. Three years later, when Margaret was hunting for a wedding dress and bemoaning all the styles, she unhesitatingly contacted Amanda. Amanda designed and sent a pattern plus satin and lace (courtesy of another cousin of Seymour's) that was transformed into a gown that was still talked about in Kennebunkport.

Days added into months, months totaled into years—women had come into and out of his life—but time and distance never eroded the relationship Lucas had with Amanda. Sample menswear still filled his closets, while Amanda had never consulted any other attorney.

Four years ago, they had celebrated the purchase of her boutique in New Orleans. "I have never signed my name so many times in my whole life." Amanda whirled around the dark, silent interior of her newly christened store on Royal Street, Rags 'n' Riches. "You made it all so easy, Lucas."

"I've got to give you credit," he lifted his paper cup of Dom Perignon in silent tribute, "your eight-year plan is right on target."

The last time he had seen Amanda was two years ago. Her phone call interrupted his work at the Dallas district attorney's office. "I need your legal mind, Crosse. The IRS sent me an I-want-you letter."

"It's a little late for them to hit you with back taxes from working at Seymour's," he had told her with a laugh. "When do they want to see you and for what year?"

"A week from Tuesday at 9:00 A.M. sharp. It's for last year. Must be the purchase of the boutique and my townhouse."

"I'll be there." He had, and as a result of his efforts Amanda had ended up with a nineteen-dollar refund from the IRS. Again they celebrated, this time on the balcony of her newly redecorated villa that overlooked Lake Pontchartrain. Lucas could still envision the gold-and-coral-ribboned sunset that mingled with the clear waters below.

"You were marvelous, Lucas." Amanda handed him a gin-laced lemonade before relaxing next to him on the cushioned redwood porch swing. "Such a glib tongue. Points of law explained without hesitation." She turned her head, the reflected crimson sky setting fire to her fog-colored eyes. "I was very impressed. What do I owe you?"

"I could use some ties." Her warm, full-bodied laugh echoed anew in his consciousness. It was strange how his memories of Amanda were always fresh, crisp, timeless—tinged with color, alive with sound and rejuvenated with emotion.

Lucas was a few seconds slower than his table companions in getting to his feet for a standing ovation. His applause, however, was the loudest and the most sincere. Amanda's fashion show was an unqualified success, and the effect of the audience's appreciation was obvious in the visible glow on her face.

To Lucas that exhilarated countenance was the essence of Amanda—the girl of his memories and the woman he encountered today. Suddenly Lucas was more determined than ever to see to it that he would be the one responsible for restoring and renewing Amanda Wyatt.

"I can't believe you didn't see Felicia drop her *pareu* on the runway. It took her three tries to pick it up. The silence was deafening!"

"You're exaggerating. No one even noticed."

Amanda twisted the key in the lock, pushing open the door that led from the garage into the kitchen. "And that replacement model, Jennifer, with the piled-high burgundy curls, she arrived with more Bourbon in her than blood. I thought she would fall off her high heels."

Lucas flicked on the wall switch, sending a shower of fluorescent light dancing across the crisp green-and-yellow breakfast room. "I couldn't tell. There wasn't a wobbly leg in the bunch." He caught Amanda by the shoulders and turned her toward him. Gone was the fiery dress and the sultry makeup, replaced by a well-scrubbed face and the modest suede outfit he had seen earlier in the day. "The major disturbance to the audience tonight was you, Amanda Wyatt. Do you have any idea what high-voltage shock waves you sent out?"

"*Moi?*" Her lashes fluttered, a gentle finger came up to twist inside the dimple on his right cheek. "Why, fiddle-deedee, Mr. Crosse," her manufactured accent duplicated

Scarlett O'Hara's, "I'm sure I wouldn't have any idea what you mean." Quite suddenly the glint in her eyes faded. "Oh, Lucas, I just couldn't believe all the mistakes tonight."

He gave her an impatient shake. "You've already forgotten that standing ovation and the endless words of congratulations, haven't you?"

Her nose wrinkled. "You should know by now that I have to complain about something. There's no learning in perfection; the challenge comes in correcting the errors the next time."

"I'm counting on the fact that you are always on the lookout for a challenge," he returned, his deep voice shadowed with a subtle hint of intrigue.

Amanda stuck out her tongue. "Go ahead, bait me, be mysterious. I'll just nag it out of you. Right now, you can keep your secret. I'm trying to decide whether to take a hot shower or make a peanut-butter sandwich. The hired help did not partake of the scrumptious fare that you enjoyed!"

Lucas aimed her toward the hallway. "Head for the showers, Mandy, and I'll make you something very gourmet. It'll give you the extra energy you need for nagging."

Warm needles of water were directed over a stiff back and shoulders. Amanda exhaled in relief under the soothing waterfall as she lathered the tension from her body. It had been a very long day and normally she would have collapsed into bed, but Lucas proved to be the vitamin pill that counteracted her malaise.

Hadn't Lucas Crosse always been the dispenser of aid and sustenance? Amanda smiled as a wave of pure affection washed over her. Lucas was her "piece of the rock," her "beacon in the night," her "life preserver"—he was all those trite, overused phrases that were the very essence of a true friend.

Amanda inched a quarter-size dollop of emerald shampoo into her palm, then sudsed life back into her dripping hair. Soap swirled down her temples, over her cheeks and under her nose. When she wiped the bitter soap from her upper lip, she thought about Lucas' moustache.

What a difference that dark wedge of whiskers made! To her designer's eye, Lucas had more visual impact. Amanda shook the water off her face and blinked rapidly. It was strange that she had never realized just how attractive a man he was. As a matter of fact, her gray eyes squinted in contemplation, she never really thought about Lucas being a man—the opposite sex!

Turning off the shower, Amanda slid open the butterfly-etched glass doors and reached for a white bath sheet. In the twelve years she had known Lucas this was the first time she had ever been conscious of his physical anatomy. Her mother had once called him "cute," but that was a decade ago, and "cute" was decidedly the wrong adjective for such heightened virility.

Amanda buffed her body with the thirsty terry, her thoughts still focused on Lucas. He was a man of many dimensions. When she had first met him in college, Lucas had been a cocky, swaggering, big man on campus, flashing his little black book and giving a *macho* analysis of every coed.

She had ignored these juvenile lapses and gradually he stopped showing off. To Amanda, Lucas' mental and emotional maturity was always the attraction. Brick by brick, incident by incident, a friendship was formed, bonded with mortar that had been able to withstand time, distance and other people. They ceased to have sexual identities. She was not a woman, he was not a man; they were confidants, comrades—each other's second self.

In the past two years, Lucas had matured even more. Age, sunlight and the moustache had weathered his features, making the "cute" face more tough, rough-hewn and compelling. His body had changed, too; his physique was more athletic, broader, stronger. The entire effect was blatantly masculine, but Lucas was more self-assured than self-centered, quiet and low-key rather than arrogant.

A primitive urge torched her body, making ruby-enameled toenails rub against the cool, oatmeal-tiled floor. Amanda hastily thrust aside the mental acknowledgment that if Lucas Crosse wasn't her best friend, she no doubt would take dead aim!

Shrill, staccato blasts pierced the air. Amanda scrambled into a lilac kimono, yanked open the bathroom door and sprinted toward the kitchen. "Lucas!" she shouted, tying the cord belt around her slender waist. "Lucas!" Amanda found him standing on a step stool, pulling the smoke detector off the wall. "How could you burn peanut butter?"

"The damn smoke alarm turned traitor. I was trying to surprise you." He kicked the metal stool into a corner, wiping his hands on the dish towel that was tucked apron like into the belt of his dress slacks. "The cheese on the eggs is brown, not burned."

Amanda inspected the contents of the plate on the stove. "We'll christen it eggs Benedict—Arnold," she said with a laugh. "You really didn't have to go to all this trouble."

"Don't be silly. Peanut butter and jelly would never go with Pouilly Fuisse." Lucas picked up a dew-kissed wine bottle from the counter, tapping the label. "Rich and full-bodied," he said, his brown gaze lingering over her tall figure draped in a column of shimmering satin, "like my hostess."

"Is that a convoluted crack about my no longer being a size eight?" Amanda admonished, not hesitating to reach for the cheese covered eggs and ham.

He handed her a knife and fork, then drew out a yellow-cushioned bentwood chair. "I always said you were too thin," Lucas reminded her, pouring the vintage nectar into twin crystal goblets.

"Hmmm," she said as she swallowed a mouthful of midnight snack. "I joined one of those health spas, and somehow the exercise program added inches and ten pounds. I must admit I do feel better."

"You look fantastic," Lucas stated, pulling out another chair. "In fact," he reached out, letting his long fingers snake through the short, damp curls, "I still can't get over how different you do look. I love the hair."

Amanda cleared her palate with wine, then leaned

closer to him, her nose butting his, her lips a scant inch from his mouth. "I'm crazy about your moustache." She relaxed back into the chair and broke into the second cheedar-covered egg yolk. "Now about this proposition?"

He swirled the contents of his glass, dimples deepening in his cheeks. "All in good time," Lucas stalled. He shifted position in the chair, his dark head inclined toward the archway. "I like what you've done. Knocking out that wall really opened up this place."

Amanda pushed her scraped plate to one side. "I really needed a dining room more than a guest room. This kitchen is tiny and I entertain a lot," she told him, her thumb and forefinger wiping her lips. "I roughed out an idea and called in an architect. He said it would be easy and inexpensive, and it was."

She peered over his shoulder and smiled. Moonlight splayed through gossamer window panels and bounced off the glass doors of the china cabinet, illuminating oriental and brass accessories on polished oak wood. "I like interior designing almost as much as fashion designing."

"You do them both with excellence," Lucas said, refilling their glasses, "but as your houseguest, I don't fancy sleeping on a serving cart."

She stood up, wineglass in hand, crooked a finger and bade him to follow. Ten steps took them into the great-room living area. Amanda's bare toe groped the floor lamp's base for a switch. The low light cast shadows against the bold raspberry walls that were tempered by the pristine white of the high ceiling. The furniture was eclectic but classic; the result was dramatic yet clean and understated. "This smooth, sleek contemporary module may look like a conversation pit," Amanda intoned, "but it also turns into a very comfortable hide-a-bed for visitors."

"In that case," Lucas gave her his best leer, "let me take you to bed." His free hand cupped her elbow, guiding her to the center section of the white Haitian cotton sofa that was splattered with rainbow-colored throw pillows.

Four long legs stretched against the matching ottoman; two bodies totally submerged themselves in comfort and tranquillity. Amanda didn't bother to adjust the ankle-length robe that slithered open to midthigh. "How much longer am I to be kept in suspense?" She slanted an amused glance.

"For a little while," he decided, clinking his wineglass with hers. "I want you in a mellow mood." Lucas' left arm formed a pillow for her neck; his long fingers amused themselves by twirling ringlets into the chestnut hair that sculpted her head.

Amanda's gray eyes inventoried his perfectly relaxed frame. The tuxedo jacket and black tie had been discarded, the pleated shirt lay open to bare half his torso, long sleeves rolled to elbows. Lucas was still wearing the dish towel-*cum*-apron, but his shoes and socks had been lost somewhere along the way.

A soft chuckle escaped her. Amanda finally put words to her laughter under the insistent tugging of her hair. "I was just thinking how easily you adjust yourself to the moment. An hour ago you were quite polished and proper and now"—her toes nuzzled against his—"you're down-to-earth, casual, right at home."

"Those new dress shoes were killing me," he reported, rubbing one foot against the other. "I knew you wouldn't mind. After all, you once paid me fifty bucks to bare these handsome toes."

"The art class paid," Amanda corrected. "I was just the procurer," she winked at him, "of various body parts to draw. As I recall, you only cooperated as far as the knees."

Lucas exhaled a dramatic sigh. "What can I tell you? I'm basically very shy and retiring."

"And I remember exactly how many female members of the art class you ended up retiring with! Ouch!" She twisted away from another sharp hair tug.

"You are still a very sassy brat," he admonished. Lucas' smile turned pensive. "Why do I get the impression your comment has little to do with feet and more to do with your previous beau?" His hand slid from her curls to her cheek, turning her face upward for inspection. "Didn't Brian Neuman ever take off his shoes?"

"Only at the proper time," Amanda returned on a dull note. "You know, Lucas, I could never put my finger on what the problem was with Brian until tonight. The man just never stopped being a doctor."

"Well, I think that's only natural," he put up a quick defense. "He probably had patients' maladies whirling through his mind, prescriptions to remember, operations to schedule, consultations—"

"Brian was a dermatologist, Lucas. Rashes and zits are not life and death." She took a final swallow, then put her glass on the sofa table. "You're a lawyer and yet you don't act the jurisconsult at every moment. You know how to adapt to your surroundings and audience."

He studied the contents of his glass. "Tell me about Brian."

Amanda's head slid into the spicy, scented curve of his neck. "I met Brian while I was putting together a Christmas fashion show for Cedars Hospital. He was about your height, sandy-haired, dark blue eyes, played racquetball. Like you, he was very easy to talk to. We started dating, hit or miss for about a month, then it became twice a week, then every day.

"You know me, Lucas. I'm . . . I'm selective. You once said God himself would have a tough time getting my undivided attention. I just never felt the need to compensate for years of female oppression. I stayed in the Victorian closet. The idea of waking up next to someone I didn't know and didn't trust made me physically nauseous."

Amanda exhaled a soft sigh. "I guess years of early conditioning and values can't be erased overnight by contraceptives and liberated mores. Maybe I'm wrong, but then I listen to my girlfriends who jump from bed to bed and they aren't all smiles either.

"Well, it took me a long, long time to feel comfortable with Brian. I liked him. He was a wonderful person and our relationship was maturing and involving. I really felt this was going to be it. We'd meet for lunch, he'd come here for dinner, sometimes stay for breakfast." She peeked at Lucas, noting a tightness in his jaw.

"Brian began to get very vocal about my business. He didn't like my buying trips, my 'artsy' friends, as he called them. I started balking, feeling stifled.

"Then I began to concentrate on the little things Brian did that bothered me and discovered there were a lot of them. We'd go to the beach and I'd get a lecture on the sunlight. We'd go on a picnic, Brian would pack the bug spray and calamine lotion and say no to a walk in the woods. Everything had to be planned, nothing spontaneous. I was getting a rash from his inspecting my pores!" Amanda gave Lucas a poke in the ribs. "Stop laughing!" she ordered gruffly.

"I was right. I think you'd even find *fault* with God," he countered. "I doubt it was anything like you're describing."

"Brian licked his coffee cup!"

"Oh, well, that's grounds for the electric chair!"

Amanda gave a snort. "I knew it wasn't going to work. We just started to drift apart. We're still friends, still have an occasional dinner or lunch. I think my mother was the most upset. To her, Brian was perfection. A doctor! Of course, she's had psoriasis for ten years. Lucas, you're laughing again!"

He swallowed hard and wiped his eyes. "I'm sorry. It's just that when I talked to your mother she said to tell you to date a plumber."

"That's because the house needs a new septic system and Dad blew up when he got the bill." Amanda shook her head. "You're lucky; men don't get stuck with the Jewish-mother syndrome."

"All mothers have chicken soup flowing through their veins. What's the difference whether its served with matzos or croutons?" Lucas gave her a sympathetic pat. "My mother worries about every woman I take a liking to and so does my father."

"He wants you to marry a girl-just-like-the-girl, et cetera."

"My mother is a dear but I couldn't marry one like her." He was thoughtful for a moment. "I need a woman who is

49

independent and doesn't need to have me around twenty-four hours a day. I also would like one with a good sense of humor and a good sense of trust and fidelity.

"When my father was going from state to state building bridges, I remember my mother's tension wondering if he was staying alone nights in the hotel rooms. But even though Mom was able to leave the three of us kids, she never took Dad up on his offer to visit any of the areas he was working. I'd like my wife to be a bit more adventurous than that."

Amanda levered herself slightly; her gray eyes studied Lucas' face. "Does Kitty Byrnes incorporate all those virtues?"

"I don't know, Mandy." He was being truthful. "I don't think six weeks is long enough to get to know a person. To be honest, Kitty and I aren't even friends yet."

"Just lovers." Again she saw his jaw tighten. Amanda smiled slightly, her feminine curves filled against his warm masculine angles. "Obviously the search for Ms. Right is just as tough as the one for Mr. Right, my friend." A tiny yawn escaped her. "How is your practice doing?"

"Being on my own is a great incentive. I'm playing the game for keeps, no going back into public law," Lucas rubbed his face, trying to hold off the invasion of weariness that threatened him. "My clients are actually paying, and I've got myself on retainer to two companies." He yawned and shook his head. "That's what I meant about finding a woman who can be happy functioning on her own. Sometimes even when I am home, my mind is on a case."

"Speaking of homes," her eyelids fluttered under a consuming burden, "the pictures you sent of all your remodeling were amazing." Another yawn interrupted. "You really turned that rambling ranch into a *House Beautiful* place."

"Well, thank you." Lucas burrowed deeper into the sofa cushions. "I'm really good at handling all the big things. You know, moving walls, building walls, sinking floors, building risers; the electricity and the plumbing weren't even a problem. It's the little things that make me shudder. The wallpaper, what colors to paint, drapes, furniture, lamps, pictures.

"Then I remembered what a beautiful job you did making your dorm room bright and cheery and the way you fixed up that loft I rented my last year in New York. Of course, this place"—his head swiveled around, a smile on his face—"this townhouse is functional and livable, but it has that classy dash and snap."

Lucas gave a low laugh. "Look at this. Without even nagging, you made me spill the beans on my proposition." He gave her a quick hug. "What do you say, Mandy? How about taking a month off—now, don't interrupt. I remember you saying the shop can get along without you. You just got through admitting how much you liked interior decorating. I've got a pretty healthy bank account set aside; you'd have fun at the ranch. I've got two horses and there's a great stream-fed pond for swimming. You can relax, meet new people. Well? Mandy? Come on, don't be bashful. Mandy?"

He finally ventured the courage to look. Instead of seeing a face wry with incredulity, he found instead that Amanda Wyatt was sound asleep!

"Some scintillating conversationalist you are, Crosse," Lucas chided. He knew he should carry her into her bedroom. But he didn't. He managed to slide their bodies into a more comfortable position without disturbing Amanda.

Lucas indulged himself, cuddling her against him. His dark eyes toured her well-curved anatomy, taking in the pleasure of her feminine form. There was a glimpse of a velvety breast beneath the lilac satin; he enjoyed the sensation of the suppleness of her slender legs and thighs between his own.

He would try again tomorrow. Lucas found there was a desperation in his thoughts to convince Amanda to come to Texas. *A desperation born of physical need,* he thought as he attempted to sleep.

Chapter Three

AMANDA'S GREEDY FINGERS broke into the warm *beignet;* she rubbed the cake doughnut in its own powdery sugar before transferring it to her eager mouth. Aromatic cups of chicory coffee dotted the bistro tables, its rich scent awakening the interest of the patrons at the Café du Monde.

The Quarter was still sleeping this crisp Saturday morning. The French Market, which displayed a staggering variety of fruits and vegetables during the week, was slowly acquiring the tenants that turned it into an addictive weekend flea market. Horse-drawn carriages began to arrive on Decatur Street. The horses' metal-banded hooves rang against the pavement in counterpoint to the whistles from the Mississippi tugboats that worked the other side of the levee.

Artists were arriving in the Vieux Carré. Amanda watched them set up their easels and hang finished paintings against the wrought-iron fence that circled Jackson Square. Standing proudly in the gardens was the magnificent bronze statue of Andrew Jackson. An ever-growing pigeon population roosted on the tail of his rearing horse. The graceful spires of St. Louis Cathedral pierced the cloudless blue sky, but multicolored umbrellas were popping open to protect against the April sun and in anticipation of the afternoon rains.

Subtle strains of accordion music tantalized Amanda's ears. The early-morning street musician was playing a melody from a Claude Lelouche film . . . very French, very mellow, very passionate. Her breakfast forgotten, Amanda leaned against the white iron chair, suddenly surrounded by fond memories.

Even though the French Quarter was dappled in sunlight and fragrant with flowers, it lacked the intimacy of Paris in winter. Strolling, chattering tourists couldn't compare with the anxious, effervescent students from the Sorbonne who filled the small cafés. While New Orleans had become a citadel for artists and sculptors, it lacked the ghosts of the old masters that haunted the crooked alleys of Montmartre.

Amanda smiled slightly. Wrapped in the blue mystery of dusk, she had walked those narrow, winding streets, that had inspired Renoir, Toulouse-Lautrec, Utrillo and Picasso. The Place du Tertre looked much like Jackson Square, filled with outdoor bistros and trees, tourists and aspiring artists amid an ever-blooming garden of easels.

A gentle breeze sent Amanda's napkin skittering along the red-checked tablecloth. She rescued the napkin, trapping the white paper beneath her coffee cup and remembered a day long ago that started the same way. It had been November and the raw wind made her drink first the apple brandy that came with her coffee; she had borrowed a Gauloise cigarette to light for warmth.

She had been very Bohemian eight years ago, very worldly, very much the artist. A student at the Chambre Syndicale de la Couture Parisienne. Amanda stayed for eight months, October to June, to train as a minor *couturière* in the *haute couture* system.

Train? Labor! By nine every morning, she and eighty other students, of varying nationalities, would squeeze onto small stools behind even smaller tables to toil until five with only a brief break for lunch. No talking was permitted during the work time. Mme. Gervaise would teach and order, walking through and ripping apart days of effort with a short, "*Non!* Like this!" A single light bulb illuminated their cramped work areas; pressing was done with flat irons heated by gas plates that Amanda had remembered seeing in the Smithsonian. The ironing board was a piece of wood on two saw horses, yet muslin patterns were always perfectly pressed.

A lot of hard work had brought her to that cramped space. She had labored mightily to attain her goal: Student Designer of the Year at the Fashion Institute of Technology. It had enabled her to go to Paris, learning from the best. She had loved it; she had cursed it. She had been happy; she had been sad. But she had never been bored.

The students had formed a solidarity group, living in a dorm, touring the city, claiming Lecole Cafe in Montmartre as their own. The outdoor bistro became their country; the students were its citizens. Amanda literally owned a wicker chair at the corner table, watching an endless parade of beautiful people who entertained with their dress.

She loved to stroll along the Place Vendôme, home of the most expensive shops on earth. She was smiled and nodded to in Nina Ricci and possessed a Hermes silk scarf. Yet on that distant November day all the breathless excitement and passion that was Paris had been forgotten, replaced with depression and despair.

In the States it was Thanksgiving. Amanda knew her parents' house would be filled with laughing relatives and friends. She could envision the golden-brown turkey stuffed with oyster dressing that would be centered on her mother's holiday lace tablecloth. Ruby-red cranberries would shimmer in their used-once-a-year crystal dish, nutmeg and cinnamon would rival all the other tempting aromas, making stomachs anxious for pumpkin and mince pies.

While there was no Thanksgiving in France, Paris was celebrating the Feast of St. Catherine, the patron saint of seamstresses and young girls. The Chambre was closed, and all *couturiers* enjoyed the holiday. Girls roamed the streets wearing their special green and yellow caps to signify their unmarried state.

If there was one city in all the world that was not meant to be viewed alone, it was Paris. Affectionate young couples strolled through Montmartre, down from the bulbous white basilica of Sacre Coeur's sacred site to Pigalle, the hotbed of the gaudiest nightlife in town.

Watching the lovers, Amanda had felt very singular indeed. She refused to join her female classmates in the rollicking Leap Year festivities that bubbled in the streets. Instead Amanda had spent the entire day in her wicker chair at Lecole's, doodling the most outrageous designs on an endless supply of paper napkins and keeping warm with a carafe of Beaujolais, crusty fresh baked bread and sizzling grilled sausages.

Late that afternoon she realized that the heady red wine had rendered her quite intoxicated; there could be no other explanation for the appearance of that familiar masculine figure that zigzagged among the outdoor tables. As Amanda's rose-tinted lips curved in a reminiscent smile, her smoky gaze suddenly became conscious that the same familiar man was headed toward her today. She repeated what she had said eight years ago in Paris: "Lucas, of all the bistros in all the world, what are you doing in mine?"

His rich laughter rose above the noise of the growing number of tourists who clustered on the sidewalk. "I read the note you taped to my toe." Lucas pulled out an ornate chair, expertly signaling for service. "You're one hell of a hostess, Mandy, leaving your houseguest on the sofa."

"You looked so cute all curled up in a fetal ball." She gave him an audacious wink. "Why didn't you wake me last night? You couldn't have been very comfortable."

He fidgeted slightly, pulling the points on the white collar of his burgundy knit shirt. "Your snoring made conversation impossible." The lie was delivered with ease. "I thought for sure you'd sleep late."

"I love coming here early on the weekends. The Quarter is closed to traffic, the artists display their paintings, the streets are filled with horse-drawn carriages. It brings back some pleasant memories."

Lucas moved his hands to allow space for the steaming mug of chicory blend and a wax-paper-wrapped *beignet*. "It does look like Montmartre." His hand reached out to tug her copper curls. "Your silly little beret is missing." He took a careful swallow of coffee; lines traversed his forehead. "I hope more than the past is pleasant for you."

Amanda shrugged, pulling absently at the elbow-length sleeve on her leaf-strewn turquoise dress. "Daydreams are always water-colored, but I was thinking how true it is that history does repeat itself." Her fingers curved in appreciation around his white-cuffed left wrist. "You showed up in Paris that November when I was depressed and homesick, and yesterday you appeared again when I needed a morale boost. How do you always know?"

"You lucked out eight years ago, Mandy." Lucas tugged his earlobe. "I was in New York. The airport in Maine was shut down due to snow. I missed the plane to North Carolina and suddenly found I needed to spend the holiday with a friend rather than strangers in the snack bar at La-Guardia."

"Liar." Amanda watched him eliminate the holeless doughnut in three substantial bites. Lucas was amazing. She knew he had canceled plans for a ski vacation in Aspen to cheer her up in Paris. And now her knight in shining armor had again arrived to rescue the fair maid.

Amanda gave him a tremulous smile, reaching out to let her fingernail dust the powdered sugar from his dark moustache. "Say, when am I finally going to hear this mysterious proposition of yours?"

"You've got a lot of nerve, kid." Lucas playfully grabbed the lapels on her V neck; the crepe de chine soothed his calloused fingers. "You fell asleep last night and missed my rather nervous dissertation."

Laughter bubbled in her throat. "Lucas, I am sorry. Tell me again." She held up her palm. "I promise not to doze off."

"I don't know," he hedged, wiping his mouth with a napkin, then neatly folding it inside the empty mug. "It may not be the brilliant scheme I first thought." Lucas found he didn't have to feign uncertainty. He was afraid Amanda would say no.

"Let me be the judge," she insisted. "Come on, while we

walk to the shop you can dazzle me with a very well-rehearsed proposal."

Arms locked together, they left the Café du Monde and headed into the Quarter. Lucas was deliberately quiet, his emotions still in a state of confusion. He had lain awake last night trying to decipher exactly why his motives had changed. Initially he had wanted Amanda to come to Dallas for a vacation, but those best laid plans were now riddled with other complications.

Amanda could no longer be his buddy, his pal or be equated with his sisters. Lucas realized his feelings had undergone a change—a change that had nothing to do with a glandular reaction to oysters or a designer gown.

The ghost of Amanda Wyatt had been an invisible specter that shadowed all his relationships. Unconsciously he had measured all women against her and found them wanting. He had even been drawn to Kitty because she was like a young Amanda.

Last night they had laughed about searching for Mr. and Ms. Right. Lucas realized the laugh was on him. He already possessed the treasure he was constantly seeking. Now Lucas felt it was essential to bring Amanda more solidly into his life. Her feelings had to change; they had to echo his own.

Amanda paused in front of the Pontalba buildings that flanked Jackson Square. "Lucas," she said, jiggling his arm, her voice low and inviting. "I won't bite your head off if I don't like your idea. Give me a chance?"

"All right, Mandy." Lucas disengaged her arm, jamming his balled fists into the pockets of his tan twill pants. "I am going to say this straight out. No sugar coating. No mincing words. No—"

"Dammit, Lucas!" Her vanilla pump stamped against his desert boot; her mouth twisted into an impatient scowl.

Laughing, he leaned against the cast-iron railing that fenced off a marigold and geranium apartment garden. "I came here to offer you a month-long vacation at my ranch. I thought you'd enjoy horseback riding, new scenery, meeting new people. I also have quite a nest egg put aside for furniture, wallpaper, paint, accessories—all the little things that will make my house a home. I know of no one who could do that better than you."

Lucas held up a peremptory finger, halting her words. "Yesterday you said, 'I'm already at my peak. I've accomplished my goals. What else is there?' " He took a deep breath, praying his logic would find favor. "I know how emotionally involved you are. It's hard to make a move away from what's safe and secure. I also know that you don't have any idea what you want to move on to. The ranch would be a perfect transition point. It could be the little step you need to identify a new challenge."

Her gray eyes surveyed his intense features. "Lucas, what a wonderful compliment. I'm deeply honored that you'd want me to contribute to your home."

Amanda scratched her cheek. "The idea of a vacation, even a working one, is appealing. But a month—" She shook her head. "That's a long time to leave the shop."

"You said yesterday that you've been coming to work and having little or nothing to do," Lucas reminded. They resumed walking, sidestepping an antique-looking popcorn wagon, the butter-coated, exploding kernels sending a fragrant message into the morning air.

"Yes, you are right." She exhaled a frustrated sigh. "I guess I just don't want it proved that I'm not needed. Dammit, Lucas, instead of adding harmony and serenity to my life you've aggravated the situation."

Amanda directed him around the corner, to Dumaine Street. "One part of me wants to rush home, throw my jeans into a suitcase and run off with you. Another part is screaming, 'Don't be a fool!' "

Lucas suddenly felt the fool. His dark gaze studied the intricate lace balconies that were the most exquisite specimens of wrought-iron work in the French Quarter. The complexity of the grill artistry reiterated the tumultuous feelings he now harbored.

Maybe he shouldn't persist. Maybe it would be more sensible to leave their relationship alone. Kitty Byrnes could be perfect for him. Amanda could stay here and work out her problems. Lucas remembered Brian Neuman. What if he came back into her life? Or someone else did?

"I think you'd be a fool not to come." His words were delivered with savage force. At Amanda's arched brow, his anger died. "Look, Mandy," Lucas bit his lower lip, the clefts deepening in his cheeks, "I want you to be happy, and I know you're not. I really believe a change is just what you need."

Amid the muted, striped awnings that graced the elegant antique shops on Royal Street stood Rags 'n' Riches. The pale coral stone building boasted a historic-site marker, commemorating its birth in 1802, when New Orleans was the capitol of the Spanish frontier of Louisiana and the street bore the name Calle Real.

Amanda had yet to acknowledge a decision, and Lucas felt even queasier as he trailed into the shop. Rags 'n' Riches was truly Amanda's child—an offspring of her personality. How could he expect her to leave it in the hands of a sitter for a month?

The boutique's tasteful but unassuming exterior gave way to an elegantly understated interior. The soothing combination of French, Oriental, and contemporary furnishings and the conspicuous absence of display racks led customers to believe they were in someone's home.

Like many specialty stores, Amanda built Rags 'n' Riches' reputation on quality merchandise and personalized service. She considered each customer to be a guest, and a guest was treated with inordinate hospitality.

The customer indicated how much was to be spent and, while comfortably ensconced on a sofa, drinking iced tea, mineral water or espresso, would be shown the appropriate fashions from the fifteen enormous walk-in closets that concealed merchandise. The customer-*cum*-guest was treated not only to an oasis of luxury and attention but to privacy as well. No customer knew how much or how little another was spending.

While there was a certain formality to the shop, Amanda's sales staff was informal and friendly. The customer who came to purchase a scarf was given exactly the same courtesy as the customer who was spending thousands of dollars on a designer gown.

"Good morning, boss." A cheery voice was heard a few seconds before a parchment-toned face fringed by blue-black hair peeked over the glass jewelry display case. "I didn't expect you this early."

"Good morning." Amanda gave her managerial assistant a preoccupied smile. "Sherry Lau, meet Lucas Crosse."

"Ah, I see yesterday's mystery man is no longer that." An inscrutable expression blanked her artfully made-up Eurasian features. "I take it he is not a pesky insurance agent."

"Lucas is definitely pesky." Amanda's smoky eyes penetrated his smiling countenance.

"Touché." He flicked her leaf earring before extending his right hand to Sherry. "I've heard so much about you. Amanda tells me that you're one of her biggest assets."

Sherry's dark, sloe-eyed gaze shifted to her boss. "Say, he's not bad"—she paused, sucking in her full cheeks—"for an Occidental."

"Lucas is launching a campaign to get me to take a vacation." Amanda gently leaned her tall frame against the glass counter. "He also wants me to decorate his ranch house in Texas."

"It sounds like a marvelous idea," Sherry agreed. One amazingly long almond-tinted fingernail scratched the curve of her jaw. She directed her attention to Lucas. "I've been trying to talk her into working half days this summer. It's our slow period."

Amanda pointedly ignored Lucas' raised eyebrow, reached for the stack of morning mail and adroitly changed the subject. "Is that Reuben's sample?" She critically assessed the cinnamon silk T-shirt that clung to her assistant's slender torso.

"Uh-huh." Sherry executed a graceful pirouette; the tunic-styled shirt-tail bottom flared over chamois slacks. "Yes?"

"You made a brilliant buy."

"Another point in my favor," Lucas quickly inserted, folding his arms in smug satisfaction across his broad chest. "Not only is Sherry perfectly qualified to manage the store, but she also knows how to purchase. Now will you say yes?"

"Maybe."

"Lucas, do you have a telephone at your ranch?" Sherry's musical voice queried with idle irony. "I could always call Amanda if there was a problem."

"Certainly, and the Dallas airport even has jets," Lucas added. The dimples forming in his sun-bronzed face belied the seriousness of his tone. "She could be back here in an hour."

Amanda cleared her throat, an I-am-not-amused expression settling on her attractive features. "It's wonderful the way you both pretend I'm not here." She hoped they would suspend any further bantering but was chagrined to discover that Lucas and Sherry had totally ignored her comment.

Concentrating on the mail, Amanda's trained eye quickly delegated a position of importance to each envelope, leaflet, brochure and catalogue. All but one could be ignored until later. She held up a large manila mailer. "This may change things."

Amanda silently digested the cover letter, then smiled. "It's from a major pattern company. They'd like to have me design a few things for next spring's line." She handed Lucas a six-page contract. "How does this look to your legal eye?"

Sherry's wide mouth twisted into a grimace that immediately turned into a smile when the small bell attached to the front door announced the day's first customer.

"It's pretty standard," Lucas told Amanda after they had adjourned to her studio in the rear of the store. Pulling a cranberry velvet-cushioned side chair next to the antique library desk, he selected a pencil from a crystal holder and checked each point.

"The money appears excellent." One dark brow lifted in

inquiry, then acquiesced to her nod. "Is the time limit acceptable?"

"Yes, but it means no vacation." Amanda leaned forward from her position on the edge of the table. Cool fingers pressed his lips together. "It also means a new challenge," she pointed out gently. "Lucas, I've never done anything like this before. It could be the perk I need."

His long fingers clamped around her slim wrist, dragging the barrier away. "There's no reason you couldn't do the designs at my place," Lucas argued, hazel eyes almost pleading. "I know you. I know you'll concentrate every waking moment on this assignment, finish it long before the due date and then aimlessly search for something else to relieve your boredom."

Amanda pulled away from his incisive gaze and began to prowl the elegantly decorated office. The cork tiles that filled the middle of one wall were dotted with fashion sketches; material swatch books were piled high in three corners; a dress form, its adjustable proportions draped in a column of emerald linen, was silhouetted in the studio's only window.

What she considered her second home suddenly seemed like a cell; her life was a prison. Everything here was safe, sane and secure. This was the end of her rainbow, her pot of gold. How could she abandon it, even for a short time?

Yet Amanda realized Lucas was right. She would totally submerge herself in the pattern company's designs. But how long would that curb her restless vitality? Adrenaline would soar, then once the project was completed, she would crash. Then what?

Hands in the pockets of her sky-toned dress, her chin pressed against her chest, Amanda stared at the burgundy and cream dragons that chased gold and beige flowers on her oriental carpet. "Let me have a week to think it over." Damn! Why was she still copping out?

Lucas leaned back in the fragile-looking but surprisingly sturdy chair. "Take all the time you need, Mandy. I had wanted to bring you back tomorrow, but perhaps you'll miss me enough not to be able to wait a week."

She bent down to pick up a dressmaker's pin that had lain almost invisibly in the carpet. "I feel so silly about making this a life-and-death matter." Amanda moved to his side, frowning into his concerned features. "I guess I'm scared, and that's a new feeling for me. I'm afraid I created an orchestra that can play a symphony without the conductor. I'm also afraid that I won't miss the music."

A comforting arm slid into the curve of her waist, drawing her close to his side. Lucas let his cheek rub against her silk-covered hip. "Listen, you know damn well you can never be replaced. You *are* Rags 'n' Riches." He found he was choosing his words with inordinate care. "I think you are in an enviable position. The people who work with you are extremely competent and trustworthy, the business is healthy, this seems the perfect time to break out and away."

Her knuckles gave a velvet tap against his head. "Lucas, are you suggesting I try a whole new career?"

He smiled up at her. "This pattern deal could be something new. So could decorating. You did mention how much you enjoyed interior designing."

Amanda's fingers absentmindedly snaked through the coils of his hair. "That's a very interesting suggestion. You know I fell into buying this store by overhearing a conversation in the line at the bank," she reminded him. "Who knows where a trip to Dallas may ultimately end."

"Just think of me as Fate's messenger," came his dry quip.

Her vibrant laughter stirred the air. Tipping Lucas' face up, Amanda lowered her own. "I love you."

He had heard her say that so many times. Today he wished it were more than an innocent declaration. The exciting scent of jasmine and roses aroused his senses. Lucas desperately craved her soft lips, anxious to sample the sweet nectar stored inside her mouth but found the kiss was a whispered gift against his slightly damp forehead. He realized his fantasies were becoming more foe than friend when it came to Amanda Wyatt. With Herculean effort, he made a silent vow to keep his emotions neutral.

Amanda looked thoughtful for a moment, then her diamond-bright eyes radiated with inner light. "Since this is your last day in the city, why don't we play tourist. You only saw the IRS office the last time you were here."

"Sounds good to me." Lucas managed an easy smile.

Her taupe leather shoulder bag slung bandelero style across her chest, Amanda led the way through the main salon. Rags 'n' Riches was relatively calm. A well-known client, in the sportswear area, raised her coffee cup in a silent toast; two other customers were busy inspecting scarves and hair accessories while Sherry was arranging a display of locally fashioned hammered silver bracelets.

"I'm taking Lucas on a tour of the Quarter," Amanda said, interrupting her assistant. "I'll call just before closing." Sherry split her fingers in a victory sign and received a hopeful smile from Lucas.

Pausing at the front door, Amanda's fingers closed over his. "Lucas, would you like to pick out something for Kitty? The jewelry Sherry is unpacking is quite lovely, and each piece is unique. It would make a—"

He shook his head. "Our relationship isn't at the gift-giving stage." The words came out in a rush. Lucas rubbed the back of his neck, trying to ease the strain. "Kitty may be nothing more than a passing encounter. I wouldn't want her to get the wrong impression."

Amanda looked at him oddly, then gave a perceptive shrug. She could readily understand his reluctance to make a commitment on the basis of a six-week relationship. After all, hadn't it taken her five months to realize that Brian was not the man for her?

Soft, warm spring air washed by a gentle gulf breeze accompanied them on their walking tour. Already the sky was thickening with black-bellied clouds, an omen of a stormy evening, and "evening" in New Orleans began after twelve noon.

They window-gazed along the shoppers' paradise that was Royal Street. Over forty antique shops were packed into the nine blocks, rendering it the country's most important antique center.

"This is a marvelous place to pick up quaint bric-a-brac," Amanda informed Lucas. She pointed to a large shiny brass spittoon. "Wouldn't that look great on the slate fireplace hearth you just built?"

Grabbing her hand, he pulled her through a bright blue painted doorway. "I'm taking this as a positive sign you'll be my interior decorator." A bank card completed the purchase—after Amanda haggled the price down seven dollars.

Her fingernails clicked against his bagged prize. "This will add a little class to your ranch."

Lucas looped his left arm through her right. "Don't you think we Texans are civilized, ma'am?" His affected drawl teased close to her ear.

"Long before Sam Houston ever dreamed about the Lone Star State, New Orleans was a sophisticated and civilized port," she parried in a lilting voice mellowed by southern charm. "We had opera and gourmet cuisine. Fashions and fine art. And . . ." Amanda stopped, jerking her companion to an abrupt halt. Her ming-blue shaded eyelid lowered in an outrageous wink. "We had sirens and sin."

Lucas tapped the tip of her straight nose. "As I recall, you were quite the sinful siren last night!"

There is a unique Old World ambience permeating the French Quarter. New Orleans is a cosmopolitan city of many moods, where the cultures of France, Spain, America, and Africa have created a singular life. Historic buildings line the narrow streets, lace iron balconies and palm fronds shade the gas-lantern-speckled sidewalks. A myriad of smells excite the senses, from the rich odor of the wharves to the seasoned aroma of the fabled Vieux Carré cuisine.

They went to Buster's for a lunch of red beans, rice and Chaurice sausages. Amanda let Lucas pay the monstrous price tag of a dollar fifty. The soul-food feast was walked off by moving with the dirge rhythm provided by the Olympia Brass Band. The colorful procession led a group of mourners to St. Louis Cemetery Number One. After a most inspirational eulogy, the band gave way to jazz, rejoicing that the deceased's earthly troubles were over.

"This cemetery has been here for over two hundred years," Amanda recounted, leading Lucas through long lanes of mausoleums. "It's never been closed and it's never been full. The vaults are used time and again."

She stopped under an aged tomb beneath a camphor tree. "Here lie the bones of Marie Laveau, a notorious voodoo queen," came her profound whisper. He watched in amazement as Amanda knelt on the concrete base and began searching the ground around the marble sarcophagus.

Her fingers triumphantly closed around their quarry—a sliver of black chalk. Her chalked cross joined hundreds of others that etched the vault. "This is supposed to bring good luck." Lucas added two crosses of his own.

Basin Street hooked into Canal, one of the widest business thoroughfares in America. Amanda expertly crossed the ten lanes of traffic to purchase a candy apple from a vendor. After nibbling off the cinnamon-spice shell, she donated the ripe fruit to a horse sporting a pink chapeau as it diligently pulled a red-wheel surry.

There was a carnival atmosphere about the Quarter. Dixieland and mainstream jazz issued from corner musicians and lone buskers. The sidewalks were crowded with people trying to make a choice between the temptation of interesting cafes and the gaudy cabarets that boasted "no cover," cheap drinks and topless/bottomless waitresses.

Hand in hand, laughing like children, Amanda and Lucas scampered onto the St. Charles streetcar, a covered haven during the cloudburst. "We have a bus named 'Desire,' " she said and grinned, settling onto a green leather seat.

He pushed the wet tendrils off her forehead. "I still feel the urge to play Brando and yell 'Stella!' "

The trolley took them to Audubon Park, skirting the antebellum homes of the garden district. Mansions dating from the mid-1800s made elegant pictures. The houses boasted graceful columns, red tile roofs and elaborate filigree work, all surrounded by perfectly landscaped gardens.

Predinner drinks were enjoyed on Pat O'Brien's Patio. Lucas added a souvenir glass from consuming an intoxicating "Hurricane" to the plastic shopping bag holding the spittoon. The setting sun made a spectacular gold and orange display in the western sky, shrouding the French Quarter in gilded charm.

The city's greatest tourist attraction, Bourbon Street, offered an interesting menu from which to choose dinner. Amanda pulled Lucas away from the open-door pleasure palaces. He wasn't alone in gawking at the exotic dancers visible inside the lurid cabarets.

Gallaoire's was the choice for dinner. They waited in a line that stretched half a block to get inside one of the Quarter's best restaurants. When Mother Nature again decided to cry, Amanda and Lucas were invited to share a huge umbrella by a very youthful elderly couple from Schenectady.

"We come back here every year on our anniversary," announced the pleasingly plump matron, who introduced herself as Connie Brisson. "Joe and I"—she snuggled her navy polyester pantsuited body against her tall, barrel-chested husband—"are celebrating fifty-three years."

Connie's keen brown eyes studied the possessive masculine arm that circled Amanda's shoulder. "I bet this is your honeymoon." Her angular face was split by a wide, knowing smile. "Aren't they a perfect couple, Joe?"

"Actually, I live here," Amanda gently corrected the woman. "Lucas is a visiting friend from Dallas."

"Oh, dear." Connie's poppy-red lips drooped. "This is the first time I've ever been wrong." She gave a disappointed sniff as her hand pulled at the damp wedge of gray hair on her nape. "You just have that honeymoon glow."

"Say," Joe's voice boomed, "what's it like here during Mardi Gras? One of these days," he said, nudging his wife, "we're going to come to the party."

"It's curb-to-curb merrymakers for the ten days preceding Shrove Tuesday, the day before Lent," Amanda dutifully recounted. "Papier-mâché sculptures, carnival costumes, gala balls and floats all pay homage to Comus, the god of revelry. Although this year's carnival was quite orderly."

"How can you call ten days of all-night partying orderly?" Lucas inquired, bumping his head against the metal spokes of the umbrella.

Amanda's silver eyes were wide, her voice innocent. "Seems normal to us—New Orleans has been doing it since 1766!"

Over a dinner of crab legs dripping with butter, Lucas found he couldn't resist making a personal comment. "You know, you do have that honeymoon glow."

Wiping her hands on her paper bib, Amanda let her index finger polish her nose. "Then I think a little powder might be needed," she teased, "but thank you, kind sir, for the compliment."

Preservation Hall was the last stop for the night. A dollar bill dropped into the basket at the front door paid the admission; two orange sodas from the soft-drink machine were an after-dinner nonliqueur. The Saturday night crowd filled benches and kitchen chairs; Amanda and Lucas were among the spill of bodies that inhabitated the floor. Portraits and photos of jazz artists adorned the walls, keeping a watchful eye on the dedicated musicians who bring so much life to the city built on a sweeping curve of the Mississippi.

"We must have walked all of ninety blocks," Lucas said and groaned, collapsing in an exhausted heap in the center of Amanda's living-room sofa.

"Poor baby." She leaned over him, soothing fingers stroking away the tired lines that etched the corners of his half-closed eyes. "And you appeared to be such a perfect physical specimen."

His hands came up to span her waist, twisting her body sideways and over until she was pressed into the nubby white cotton cushions by his muscular frame. "I had an absolutely wonderful day." Lucas' deep voice caressed her ear, his face burrowed into the scented hollow of her neck.

"I'm glad and I'm very glad you came." Amanda turned her head, finding their faces were only a nose length apart.

"You know something, Lucas," she said quietly, as sadness reshaped her mouth, turning her lips into a rose-tinted *moue,* "I'm going to miss you terribly."

"Then come back with me." He spoke with urgent determination. "Make it just a vacation, even for a week." Lucas found he was blurting disjointed phrases that were actually private dreams. "I feel that I'm just getting to know another side of you, and I don't want to let go."

Her smoky eyes blinked in confusion. "Lucas, that's an odd thing to say. I'm me. I'm the same person I have been for the past twelve years. There is no other side!" Amanda shook her head and laughed. "I think you've really had too much sightseeing." She gave him a playful shove that landed him on the navy and beige Persian carpet.

"Why don't you take a shower while I make up your bed?"

Lucas did—a very long cold one.

Sniffles and coughing and one lone hiccup made Lucas shake his head. "I don't remember you crying this much when you saw me off at Orly in Paris."

Amanda blotted her eyes on the corner of his borrowed handkerchief. "I know," she said and sighed, giving him a shaky smile. "I just hate saying good-bye. You're so nice to have around." Her upraised palm stopped his words. "Don't worry, I'm still considering your proposition."

"Good." Lucas shifted his carry-on bag, somehow managing to let his left hand hold it and the shopping bag from yesterday's bargain hunting. His right hand took possession of Amanda's elbow. "I'm trying a very important case in two weeks. I'd love to have you see your barrister in action."

"It's too bad we're not in England," she remarked with thoughtful consideration of his tall, broad-shouldered physique. "You'd look marvelous in a black robe and powdered wig."

"I look marvelous," he mimicked, "in that charcoal suit you sent." Lucas privately thought Amanda looked marvelous in her snug-fitting jeans and pewter-tone sweater.

A disembodied voice announced the final boarding call for his flight. "Well, boy"—she inhaled an expressive breath, busying herself by straightening the placket on the bronze knit shirt she had given him—"I do hate to see you fly off. Thanks for caring enough to come."

Lucas became mesmerized by twin crystal irises. He had a million things he wanted to say but this wasn't the time or the place. Long fingers cupped her pointed chin. "Take care of yourself." His words were gruff, almost harsh—in total contrast to the delicate kiss he pressed against Amanda's half-parted lips.

A rainbow-striped catamaran pierced the sunrise haze that enveloped Lake Pontchartrain. Amanda watched the catamaran disappear into the crimson-edged fog as her fingertips removed the noseprint she had left on glass panes of the French balcony door.

The rooms in her townhouse seemed strangely vacant despite the colorful, eclectic furnishings. She was feeling very lonely—even more so than before Lucas had arrived. Lucas!

His prediction had been true. For the past few days she had let Sherry take care of Rag 'n' Riches while she stayed home and planned her first pattern design. It had been exhilarating to create something from nothing. Rough penciled sketches littered the floor until a final choice was made.

Amanda had decided on a blazer, the body lightly fitted, a mandarin-style collar, welt pockets and sleeves that could run the gamut from capped to wrist-length depending on the consumer's whim. Her sketch turned into a paper pattern, which she then shaped into a muslin practice piece. Amanda had run up a sample of the blazer in jade linen. The effect was stunning, and the pattern was quite easy for a home sewer to follow. She had mailed each step and detailed instructions to the company. Now—now things were just as before.

Not quite. Amanda flopped into the rattan lounge chair near the fireplace. Her gray eyes traced the complicated filigree work of the gold peacock fan that replaced logs during the warm-weather months. She found she was thinking more and more about Lucas. Her best friend invaded her thoughts night and day.

They had drifted in and out of each other's lives over the years, and yet this time Lucas' presence seemed more intense, more crucial. Or was she just wishing? Amanda hadn't thought about it before, but Lucas Crosse was a very important person in her life.

How many times had she made mental notes comparing Brian Neuman to Lucas? How many times had Brian, and a few others, ever measured up? Not many! But wasn't that natural? Didn't most women compare one man to another? Lucas had spent more time actively participating in her life than her father had. So wasn't Lucas the natural choice for comparisons?

Pushing herself from the chair, Amanda ended up sprawling face down on the sofa. She didn't bother to dig out from under the avalanche of colored throw pillows that buried her white terry-robed body. They had fallen asleep on this couch, Lucas' rugged body sculpted against her soft curves.

She looked at her hand, remembering the strength of his calloused fingers as they curled around hers, pressing them against the dark mat of hair that furred his chest. Amanda even remembered the crisp citrus scent of his skin and the silly way the dish towel he had used as an apron made him look even more masculine.

Idly, she wondered what Lucas would be like as a lover. Slow and thoughtful, patient and tender? Or would he be wild and rough, quick and selfish? Somehow both appealed. A purely feminine reaction snaked through her body, starting low in the stomach, twisting its aching sensual message into every fiber.

Without a second thought, Amanda inched forward, letting her fingers capture the telephone receiver. Eleven numbers later, the object of her lust sleepily answered the phone. "Lucas, it's Amanda. I'll be there on Sunday."

Chapter Four

THE TWO WOMEN made a rather odd couple as they came hand in hand through the airport gateway. One was tiny in stature, in her early fifties with a modern, navy-toned nun's habit cloaking her angular frame. The other was tall, twenty years younger; her shapely figure was molded by a beige safari-styled pantsuit. The only thing they appeared to have in common were the water stains that marked their clothing.

Lucas shook his head and smiled. "Mandy!" One large hand waved in the air, competing for her attention over the noisy crowd that jammed the arrival gateway.

Amanda gave the nun a good-bye hug and angled toward him. "Hi!" Her wide, toothy grin was an understatement of the amusement glinting in her eyes.

"What kind of trouble did you get into on the plane." It was a statement, not a question. Lucas took her canvas and leather carry-on, then led the way through the congested hall.

"It wasn't much . . . not really." Her eyes were wide and innocent, her expression serious. "Although Sister Felicia and I did get a round of applause from our fellow passengers."

"Oh, God."

"*He* was on our side." Amanda's sober tone was demolished by a burst of giggles as she locked her arm into his. "I loved it, Lucas. It was truly a giant step for mankind.

"The sister was next to the window, and I had the aisle seat. The gentleman, and I use the term loosely, between

72

us should have flown first class or cargo because his bulk draped onto our cushions.

"He was a disgusting specimen, Lucas." Her voice became grim. "After making a few rude comments to me and grunting at the nun, he ordered two bottles of Scotch, opened them both and proceeded to drink them at the same time. Then he had the nerve to light up a cigar that was rolled yesterday in someone's cow field.

"I politely reminded him that he was in the no smoking section. He puffed even harder. Sister Felicia turned green. I told him to snuff his butt. He growled an expletive deleted. The sister turned purple. I saw red and torpedoed his nickle stogie into his drink.

"He bellowed like a bull moose, jumped up, forgetting his seat belt was still fastened, jarred the table and sent the drinks exploding over everyone. The stewardess relocated him." Amanda's contented sigh was nearly drowned out by Lucas' laughter. "It was marvelous and it seems an omen that my vacation will not be boring." She looked at the seemingly endless corridor that still lay ahead and jogged his arm. "Lucas, I know Texas is big, but isn't this going a bit too far?"

"Our psychiatric population has soared since they built this airport," came his dry rejoinder. "Passengers have been known to suffer nervous breakdowns racing from one terminal to another trying to catch their flights."

Lucas stopped walking, turned and caught Amanda's chin between his long fingers. The sienna curls were in charming disarray. Her complexion was flushed by her adventure; her eyes glowed like twin solitaires. She looked like a mischievous child, the freshman rascal who invaded his life twelve years ago. It seemed like old times. Natural and easy.

He found he was more relaxed in her presence. The sexual tension that had possessed his body had been broken. Had it just been a *macho* fantasy, or was it because he had seen Kitty this week? Damn! Who said women were more fickle than men? A soft smile etched his face. "I'm really glad you decided to come."

Amanda's diamond-bright gaze strayed over the lean, muscular length of him. Lucas looked every inch the cowboy in his western plaid shirt, slim-fitting jeans, silver-buckled belt and leather boots. While it had been a carnal image that prompted her visit, she realized that Lucas' attraction had little to do with biology and more to do with trust, honesty and a symbiotic relationship that benefited both parties. "I'm glad I'm here too."

"This can't be all the luggage you brought." He lifted the small suitcase.

"Yup. Just a pair of cut-offs and a T-shirt to paint in, a handful of casual clothes and one dress in case you decide to take me out for gourmet chili." She rubbed the stains that decorated her twill-covered thighs. "I hope you own a washer!"

The powerful late-afternoon sun hammered their eyes into slits and contorted their smiles as they made their way through the car-infested parking area. "Well, what do you think?" Lucas stopped next to a battered Datsun truck, its short bed filled with plywood and two-by-fours.

"Where's your beige Fiat?" Amanda cried, grimacing at the white, rust-freckled vehicle. "Don't tell me you wear that Pierre Cardin suit in this thing!"

"I still have the Fiat." As he pulled open the cab door, the hinges emitted a squeaky greeting. "But this," Lucas gave the aged metal an affectionate rub, "this is—"

"A piece of junk," she offered hopefully.

He ignored her crass comment and gave her a helping hand into the masking-taped red cloth seat. "You can insult a man's job, you can insult a man's mother but never, ever insult a man's car," Lucas intoned in a deep, warning voice.

"Well," Amanda drawled, shifting her feet to accommodate the suitcase, "at least I can now truly claim I've been picked up in a pickup."

With consummate ease, Lucas extricated the truck from the center of the Metroplex, negotiating the monstrous maze of freeways that connected from the north exit. "How did your pattern project turn out?"

Amanda stuck her tongue out at his chiseled profile. "You know me too well, Lucas Crosse." She slunk down against the bench seat and stared at the traffic-choked highway. It seemed Texans were preoccupied with the internal-combustion engine. "I ended up doing exactly what you predicted," she grudgingly admitted. "I worked night and day and got the design, the pattern and the sample fashioned in record time.

"Then I was back to where I started. Nothing to do at the shop so I stayed home, stared out the window, counted raindrops and sighed a lot." Amanda twisted sideways in the seat, knuckles extended to caress the curve of his jaw. "It's going to be up to you to make sure I'm not sighing and staring in two states!"

"Listen, kid," Lucas said and flashed her a roguish grin, "I've got a clear, spring-fed pond, two complacent horses that love to be ridden and an eight-room house just screaming for your talented hand."

The swiftly rushing air became sweet as the scent of mown grass replaced the carbon-monoxide fumes. Amanda's eyes widened in delight at the explosion of wild flowers that traversed the concrete artery. It was as though an artist had dipped his brush into a multicolored palette; the gold and crimson, orange and purple fields brought the land to life. "This is lovely. How far from the city are we?"

"About twenty miles. The ranch is just outside of Farmersville but you'll have to go into the Dallas shopping centers to get your decorating supplies," Lucas added with dutiful consideration. A dimpled grin punctuated his features. Laughing hazel eyes slanted away from the windshield. "I'll leave you the keys to the truck."

A low groan assailed his ears. "At least it's an automatic."

The pickup was directed off the highway onto a dirt road. "This gives me a wake-up massage every morning!" Lucas yelled, trying to make his words heard over the creaking shock absorbers and the bouncing, shifting cargo.

Then, suddenly, dirt packed and smoothed the potholes, and the rocks disappeared. Amanda was greeted by a cool grotto of mesquite trees, a sun-toasted, stucco ranch-style house at the cusp of the crescent drive. "Oh, Lucas," her fingers gripped his tempered biceps, "I can see why you snapped up this place. It's beautiful."

The powerful diesel engine came to a halt. "The exterior and grounds promised a lot more than the interior delivered," he related, leading her through an arched entryway into a concrete courtyard. "The previous owners had let the place fall apart. Walls were punched full of holes, floors were riddled with termites and the plumbing was so antiquated that an outhouse would have been a step up."

Lucas unlocked the front door. "I loved the property, which was what I was really after. I saved the block shell and the arched windows and literally rearranged the insides." He took a deep breath, then suddenly smiled. "Why do I feel I should carry you across the threshold?"

Amanda laughed. "Here, carry this." She handed him her suitcase and stepped inside.

The earth-tone slate foyer gave way to a stunning multileveled L-shaped living area. A natural stone fireplace was built on an inside corner; its double hearth served both the main room and a large windowed and bookshelved alcove that was on the highest riser. Arched windows provided light and a stunning view of treed, rolling acres. The walls were unfinished, the wallboard spackled and taped, ready for finishing touches; the floors were alternately dark and light squares of polished teak.

Amanda wandered into the dining area that connected with a remodeled kitchen. The gold-toned appliances and butcher block cabinets gave the room a warm, inviting glow. Sliding glass doors led to a wrap-around terrace that was also accessible from the living room.

The bedrooms were at the far end of the house. The smallest was still under construction, pink rolls of insulation visible between the strutting. The middle guest room contained a double bed, a small dresser and a chair, the same sparse furnishings that were housed in the master bedroom.

"Well?" A wealth of anxiety tinged that one word. Lucas

peered over Amanda's shoulder, his dark gaze searching her intense features reflected in the oatmeal-toned bathroom's vanity mirror.

Smiling at their double image, Amanda reached back to capture and soothe the twitching masculine fingers that curved around her shoulders. "I'm really quite speechless. The photos you sent didn't give you your just credit." Her tone reflected her awe. "Lucas, you've done an incredible job. The house is stunning."

Amanda's lips quirked upward; she leaned back, using his broad frame for support. "But what on earth have you been sitting on? Except for the bedrooms, and they are pretty sparse, there's not a stitch of furniture in here—not even the proverbial orange crate!"

As Lucas rested his chin on her shoulder, the scent of lilacs whispered to him. "There are a couple of homemade barstools in the kitchen. I did have a sofa and a couple of chairs and two orange crates but"—he grinned, his voice warm and low in her ear—"I spent all day yesterday housecleaning and trucking that stuff to the dump. I figured if I played on your maternal instincts, you wouldn't leave until this place was completely habitable."

She tapped his nose. "Wait until you get my bill for decorating services!"

"You can take it out in trade," came his teasing rejoinder.

Amanda followed him back into the living room. "I've got to admit I'm finding this quite an exciting challenge." Slowly she made a three-hundred-sixty-degree turn. Her accomplished designer's eyes appraised the light that was refracted off the white-textured and natural-beamed ceiling and judged the shadows that were cast against the walls.

She had always likened personalities to colors. Aggressive and bold, quiet and unassuming, flashy and flamboyant, muted and dull—each had a definitive hue.

Long ago she decided Lucas was a neutral. Not that he was boring or bland, rather he was the epitome of the scales of justice that symbolized his profession—impartial, objective, tolerant and fair-minded. Neutral could run the gamut from creams to beige to terra-cotta to rich wood tones. A house that was earthy and natural, rustic and a bit rough-hewn with a splash of bright here and a little greenery there. That would be a home to Lucas Crosse.

"Here we go." He placed a tall glass filled with ice and lemonade into her hand. "I thought we'd eat barbecued chicken while watching the sunset. There's patio furniture on the back terrace."

"Hmmm." Amanda's tongue circled her lips. The lemonade was spiked with gin and limes and tartly refreshing. "How about showing me your two horses. I haven't been riding since . . . since I was fifteen and we were stationed in Kentucky." She took another healthy swallow of the pulp-laden liquid. "Lucas, I don't think you've ever mentioned your horses' names."

"I was too embarrassed," he finally admitted while they walked along a dirt path carved through ankle-high grass. "The mares were from a 4-H project and were already christened when I bought them."

The four-stall rough wood barn did double duty as a garage and stable. The Fiat convertible, its polished brown body belying its seven-year age, sat next to a small riding mower and assorted garden equipment.

"You've really become the gentleman farmer," Amanda remarked, the fragrant odor of hay, saddle soap and leather enveloping her.

A double whinny and the sound of pawing hooves broke through the shadowy calm. "This is Buttercup and this is Maizey." A lopsided grin twisted Lucas' face. "They've got a very comfortable running walk and a smooth canter."

Amanda cooed in delight at the saddle horses, their chestnut coats shined with well-cared luster. Maizey's head bobbed in a friendly greeting; only the white blaze on her forehead kept the two horses from looking like twins.

"Game for a little ride?" Lucas inquired.

Amanda was already rolling up the sleeves on her jacket. "Try and stop me."

She paid close attention to the saddling instructions.

First came the red-and-black-checked blanket, then the western saddle. Maizey stood quietly while Amanda fumbled with the cinch strap and added a bit of length to the stirrup. Taking the reins, she followed Lucas through the back gateway into the open air.

It had been fifteen years since Amanda was on a horse, but riding was a talent instantly recovered. Her low-heeled Oxford caught the metal stirrup, her right leg was thrown across the horse's back. She settled in a relaxed position, her weight settled firmly in the dip of the saddle, her spine erect but not stiff.

"Not bad, kid, not bad." With infinitely more grace and precision, Lucas duplicated Amanda's effort. Both riders squeezed their legs against their mounts' sides, letting their reins follow the movement of the horses' heads. "I'll take you to the pond. That way you'll know how to ride out during the day."

They started out at a walk, then as Amanda began to remember how to use her hands, legs and body weight to cue Maizey, the gait increased to a two-beat trot, then shifted to a comfortable, three-beat rhythmic canter.

"How are you doing?" Lucas called, ever watchful of the variable terrain.

"I'm claiming the bathtub while you fix dinner!" Amanda yelled, her saddle creaking under the shifting weight of an uncomfortable posterior. "Where is this pond—in Arkansas? We must have ridden fifty miles!"

"Only three," Lucas reigned Buttercup and waited for Maizey and her grumbling rider to join them. "There it is."

A field vivid with orange Indian paintbrushes and stately bluebonnets sloped into a pond ringed by luxuriant foliaged cottonwood trees. The tranquil, subtly moving water mirrored the rainbow-stained western sky, the sun a slowly lowering fiery ball on the horizon.

"I hope this is not a mirage." Amanda's tone reflected the pastoral beauty.

"Wasn't this worth a few saddle sores?" he teased, leaning over to possess her left hand. "That's why I fell in love with this place, Mandy. The sheer majesty of nature. Restful, peaceful . . . a haven away from the workday grind and the city grime."

Her smoky gaze shifted to study his face, exploring the rugged planes and angles she knew so well. "Lucas, at times you are very poetic and profound." Amanda was quiet for a moment. "What happened to that intense attorney of a few years back who was so anxious to carve his name in the annals of jurisprudence?"

He gave a shrug, eyebrows pulling together at the bridge of his nose. "I think everyone dreams about making a niche in time, taking history and weaving his personal thread through it." Lucas leaned back in the saddle, looping the reins over the horse.

"For six years I worked in the DA's office. It was like working in a human junkyard. Murders, rapes, hookers, pimps, drugs. It made me angry and mean. I didn't like myself; I didn't like the system. I knew I couldn't change the system, but I could change me.

"My private practice is basically civil cases and corporate law. I'm more content. Working around the house and land has reduced my anger. You know something, Mandy," his expression was serious, "I don't know how I ever lived all those years in semifurnished apartments with the corner park the sole custodian of the trees and flowers."

Buttercup and Maizey pawed and whinnied at the scent of fresh water. Cued toward the pond, the horses plodded through the fuzzy cottonwood seeds, sending a fantasy snow shower over their riders. The trip back was done at a gallop that Amanda found slightly more painful. When they returned to the barn, she pointedly ignored Lucas' teasing comments and headed for a long, hot soak in the bathtub.

Rustic twig furniture and bandanna placemats gave the terrace a casual, down-home appeal. Succulent chicken glazed with honey and barbecue sauce sizzled on the bricked charcoal grill. Amanda purloined a crouton from the Caesar salad and eagerly embraced another spiked lemonade before settling onto the padded comfort of a sturdy chaise longue.

"There you are," Lucas came out of the house, a serving plate and tongs clutched in one pot-holdered hand. "How's the body?" His chestnut eyes penetrated the saffron light to inspect her supine, navy jumpsuited figure.

"The body is starving," she intoned, watching him expertly transfer the braised fowl from grill to platter. Despite his backyard chef duties, Lucas looked crisp and fresh in tan denims and a loden green knit shirt. Dark coils of shower-damp hair sculpted his virile head. The musky scent of his cologne reiterated the earthy outdoors.

"Drag your body over here," he directed, moving past her to the small round dining table. Two willow chairs scraped against the concrete flooring, and a large citronella candle flamed to life.

"Delicious!" Amanda sucked the rich barbecue sauce from her fingertips. "You're going to spoil me."

Lucas filled two individual wooden salad bowls and passed one to her. "You don't think I'm going to do all the cooking while you're here. I had high hopes of coming home to some mouth-watering southern specialties." Voracious teeth tore at a meaty thigh.

Amanda dug into her crisp salad. "Why do I get the feeling my new occupation in life is going to be that of housekeeper?" Her empty fork stabbed the air. "I'm going to be slaving all day over a bucket of paint and you expect pecan pie with a crust that melts in your mouth!"

"Ohh, that's so unfair, Mandy," Lucas said and groaned, wiping his hands on a large paper napkin. "You know pecan pie is my favorite. Couldn't you make just one?"

The little-boy quality in his voice made Amanda laugh. "I'll think about it." She reached for another chicken leg.

The crimson and coral sunset was being rapidly absorbed by an indigo banner. Night sounds serenaded them—crickets, cicadas and an occasional owl ruptured the quiet with their songs. Hunger appeased, Amanda abandoned eating, her attention captured by the single

star that held court in the sky; the fabled prairie moon was
nowhere to be seen.

"Where are you?"

Lucas' voice seemed a long way off. "Wishing on a star."
Amanda rested her chin on updrawn knees. "Lucas, what
do you see for yourself in the next few years?"

"More philosophy?" His plate pushed aside, forearms
flat on the table, he carefully considered her question. "I'd
like to see my practice mature and stay healthy. I'm not
immune to a modicum of financial security."

"That's business," she interrupted. "What about per-
sonal?" Amanda stared at his candle-illuminated features.
The night shadows and the flickering orange flame cast
Lucas in Halloween retrospect.

"You women don't have a monopoly on parental instincts," he said at length. "I'd like to turn that small bedroom into a nursery. The problem comes in finding the
right lady."

"Are you still seeing Kitty?"

Lucas picked up a teaspoon and poked at the ice in his
drink. "When I came back last week, I felt shaky about
Kitty." He took a deep breath, eyes still concentrating on
the droplet-covered glass. "You had a lot to do with that."

Amanda's forehead puckered. "Me?"

"Yes, you." He gave a self-conscious laugh and suddenly
wished he had never tacked on that last remark. "Do you
realize that my relationship with you is the longest sus-
tained relationship I've ever had with a woman? You do
tend to overshadow other ladies."

Her bare feet slapped against the concrete. "Well, since
we seem to be playing the truth game"—Amanda cleared
her throat—"do you realize that ours is the longest sus-
tained relationship I've ever had with a man? And you,
too, Lucas, tend to overshadow other males. Silly, isn't it?"

"Yeah, silly." Lucas took a healthy mouthful of lemonade and found the gin had settled on the bottom. He
coughed. "Kitty's anxious to meet you. She's having a
cocktail party either Friday or Saturday, and you're invited."

"I'm anxious to meet her too." Amanda's fingertips drummed against the tabletop. "Listen, Lucas . . . I . . . I don't want to cramp your style. You can always give me a quarter and send me to the movies."

"Cute," came his dry retort. "I think I'll just send you to the kitchen to clean up. I've got a brief to look over for court tomorrow." Lucas tossed his napkin into his dish. "Plan on spending Wednesday with me in town; I want you to see my new office."

Amanda began to organize the table. "Sounds good. I can go furniture hunting." Licking her lips, palms rubbing together: "It's going to be so much fun spending your money." She pointedly ignored Lucas' tortured moan.

The kitchen made work a pleasure. The major appliances formed an efficient triangle, the sink aerator quickly gobbled the garbage while the dishwasher eliminated a previously soapy, time-consuming but necessary chore.

Amanda found her thoughts focused on decorating. Rummaging through the ever-present kitchen junk drawer, she found a note pad, pencil and folding carpenter's ruler. She measured carefully to find out how much wallpaper would be needed to fill the gap between the countertop and the cabinets and to cover the narrow area that surrounded the sliding glass doors. Drapes and rod length were also calculated.

The teak flooring in the living room and alcove was much too beautiful to be completely covered, yet some type of carpet would be needed—perhaps an oriental. Amanda jotted down ideas for paint colors, fabrics and furnishings. Her papers became filled with measurements and sketches. She wondered how Lucas would feel about filling the arched windows with hanging plants—greenery that wouldn't require too much of a bachelor's attention.

Two hours later, Amanda found herself peering into the master bedroom. "You are going to need a home office or, at the very least, a desk," she stated, surveying the books, papers and file folders that littered his bed. "Is this where you usually work?"

Lucas tossed his pen into a law book to mark his place. "Hey," he gave her a cocky grin, "I've done some of my best work in bed."

"Now who's being cute?" Her laughing gaze investigated the odd tilt to his mattress. "Lucas," her tone was piqued with interest, "exactly what kind of bed do you have?"

His eyebrows wiggled suggestively. "Step into my parlor," invited his deep voice. "This was a bonus from my very first client." Lucas dangled a white plastic switch just out of reach. "It's adjustable and it vibrates."

Amanda exhaled a low whistle. "Sounds better than a ride at Disneyland. Move over!" She slid onto the chocolate-brown sheets and grabbed the control. There were six buttons, three for each side of the king-size bed. Amanda blithely pressed them all.

The lower half began to rise along with the top. Papers and books bombarded their bodies. The mattress formed a V. The last two buttons added a restful massage against their contorted spines. "This is great!" Amanda exclaimed. The bed lowered their heads but kept their feet elevated. "I love it."

"Mandy, you're going to send us to a chiropractor if you keep this up." Lucas exhaled in relief when his legs were allowed to resume their correct position.

Wiggling into the downy softness, Amanda luxuriated in the vibrating fingers that tingled against her horizontal curves. "I think it would be quite fitting if you gave your guest this marvelous bed."

"Dream on, kid." Lucas began to re-sort his fallen papers. "How do you like the house?"

"There's nothing not to like." Amanda reached for the notes she had tossed on the small nightstand. "I was thinking about stucco for the living-room walls. I did that in my dining room and it looked great."

"Mmm. I remember. Sounds good."

"How would you feel about ferns instead of drapes? Those windows are just too gorgeous to cover up, and there's no one to look in. You'll just have to water the plants and say something pleasant once a week."

Lucas laughed. "I can handle that."

"I was also thinking the alcove would be a perfect spot for a desk. You can fill the shelves with law books and even a small file cabinet." Amanda turned her head, the copper curls glowing rich against the brown percale.

"I knew you'd make an excellent interior decorator." His thumb and forefinger plucked a white thread off the shoulder of her terry romper. "I'm going to need a dresser and chifforobe in here and some things for the guest room. My folks will be coming for Thanksgiving." Lucas leaned across Amanda, and his hand searched inside the nightstand's drawer. "This," he dropped a blue checkbook on her stomach, "is a special account I opened yesterday. I told the bank your name would be the signature."

Gray eyes widened at the healthy balance. "Lucas, you certainly know how to make a lady happy."

He was suddenly serious, and his long fingers stroked the curve of her jaw. "I do want you to be happy, Mandy. Take one day at a time. Have fun. You're supposed to—"

"I'm supposed to use this time for R&R." The pads of her fingers followed the grooves in his cheek, then bounced lightly against his chin. "Rest and reorganization." Amanda smiled. "It's funny, Lucas, but I feel exhilarated, happy, excited. I'm very glad you came up with this idea."

"And being a city girl, you don't think you're going to go crazy out here in the country?"

"Don't I have that great pickup to drive into town?" Her lips gave a humorous twist. She observed his intense manner. "Why is my woman's intuition telling me that your question has a double edge? Is Kitty a city girl?"

Lucas nodded and dropped back against his bed pillow. "Believe it or not, it was Kitty who sold me this property last year. That's how we met, although I didn't really get into a relationship with her until three months ago."

"Well, if Kitty sold you the house . . ."

"She tried to talk me out of it. Kitty saw a rundown ruin in the middle of weeds."

"But surely with all the remodeling you've done . . ."

"I don't know, Mandy." He winced and rubbed his face. "Kitty really gets off on the city. She loves the hustle and confusion, thrives on the pressure and embraces all the glamor. She does have a few . . . attitudes that annoy me."

"And you're so perfect, Mr. Crosse." Amanda's tone was light.

"Hardly." He came up on one elbow. "But as you pointed out with Brian Neuman, it's those little things that fester and infect a relationship. I keep waiting for Kitty to grow up. But she's stubborn." His dark eyes slanted toward his companion. "She does remind me of you in that respect."

"Me!" Amanda rallied with loud indignation. "Stubborn! You've got some nerve!" She yanked the pillow from under his head and pummeled him with foam punches. "Take that back, Lucas Crosse!"

Laughing, he easily struck aside her weapon. Strong hands pinned her shoulders flat against the mattress. "Stubborn and opinionated." His faced loomed close, eyes locked in humorous combat. "Hostile and obstinate."

Amanda's hands splayed against his muscular torso, her fingers captured amid the dark curls that were freed by his partially unbuttoned shirt. "You make me sound like a shrew." Her pink tongue poked a childish response.

"Never a shrew, Mandy." Lucas felt his body grow hard with desire, his chest eagerly seeking the softness of her breasts. Once again he discovered how easy it was to forget that Amanda was his very best friend.

"Lucas!" She gave him a playful tap against his cheek. "You're crushing me! All this remodeling has turned you into Charles Atlas!" Amanda found herself released from her masculine prison. Rolling off the bed, she displayed an exaggerated crooked swagger toward the door. "I'll take my broken decorator bones to my own flat, uninteresting bed."

Chapter Five

AN INCESSANT SEQUENCE of high-pitched beeps punctured Amanda's sleep-engulfed subconscious. She sat bolt upright in bed, thinking her microwave had gone berserk, the oven ready to self-destruct.

Gray eyes blinked in momentary confusion at the unfamiliar surroundings. This stark, rough-walled, sun-shadowed room was not the Georgian furnished master bedroom suite in her New Orleans townhouse.

The sonorous tones continued. Throwing off the geometric blue sheet, Amanda stumbled across the hall, following the sounds into Lucas' bedroom. There on the water-ringed nightstand was the source—a modular brown telephone. "Hello." Her greeting was accompanied by a prodigious yawn.

"Damn! Did I wake you?"

"Lucas?" She yawned again, shook her head and wiped the wetness from her eyes. "What time is it?" Her tongue washed over her teeth.

"Ten."

"I haven't slept this late in years." She rolled onto his neatly made bed, her free arm and both legs extended in a wakeful feline stretch. "You should have pounded on my door before you left for the office."

"Mandy, you're on vacation. I could kill myself for calling. Go back to bed and sleep till noon." Lucas' deep voice issued the tender order.

"I think," her hand groped along the padded headboard, fingers curling around the switch that controlled the vibrator, "I'll just lie here between your sheets and let your mattress give me a morning massage."

His throaty laugh caressed her ear. "I wish I could join you. I'm headed into court in another hour and . . . oh-oh . . . the other phone line is flashing." His parting statements were delivered in a rapid staccato. "I'll be home around six. I left the truck keys next to the checkbook on the counter. Have fun. Bye."

Amanda listened to the dial tone's serenade for a long moment. *I wish I could join you*—Lucas' words echoed in her mind, making her think of last night.

They had shared this very bed. Laughing and talking just as they always had. Natural, easy, unrestricted. But at some point, while they were wrestling, Amanda found she was responding to Lucas' silly play the way a woman reacts to a man. She provoked and flirted. Not just with words, but with her body as well. And she had enjoyed it.

Her cheek nuzzled the brown linen pillowcase, her nose inhaling the subtle souvenir left by Lucas' spicy cologne. Gray eyes closed against Monday morning reality. Amanda's emerald nightgowned body luxuriated in the oscillating delights of the mattress; her thoughts drifted and darted in unrestricted abandon.

She found it was very easy to respond to sensual illusion. The weight of Lucas' flat torso again pressed into her softly rounded stomach; her long legs were spread by an invisible pair of firm athletic thighs.

Nipples formed twin peaks beneath their satin cover in much the way they had taunted the rugged masculine chest that teasingly sought to conquer. Her breathing came hard and fast, just as it had last night. And again it had nothing to do with game-playing energy.

Amanda sat up, rudely interrupting her erotic fantasy. "This is silly. We were just joking. We've done it before." Her voice, loud and sensible, sent a wave of embarrassed color across her skin. The massage unit was switched off, the sheet and blanket straightened and one female body was marched into the bathroom. Halfway through a brisk shower, Amanda found her seductive musings gurgled down the drain.

The silence was total. Not even a bird. The crisp, astringent air cleansed and energized her soul. Amanda grinned like a truant kid; her navy espadrilles kicked the stones off the back patio. Coffee mug in hand, she wandered down to the stables to check on Buttercup and Maizey. Both horses were quietly munching their breakfast hay, chestnut tails and ears twitching away the pesky barn flies.

The *Morning News* was stuffed in the rural delivery box. Amanda settled at the terrace picnic table, perusing the front page and reading local stories. A paint sale in nearby McKinney caught her attention.

She made a call to the hardware store to make certain they carried stucco paint. A rueful expression twisted her lips when she found the price was two dollars a gallon cheaper than she had paid when she did her own home. Directions in hand, Amanda unhesitatingly clambered into the Datsun pickup and headed into town.

Two hours later, the short-bed truck was the transporter not only of paint, painting tools and borrowed wallpaper sample books but also potted ferns, hanging baskets, indoor trees, potting soil and clay pots. Amanda had found a highway nursery going out of business.

Denim wrap skirt and white knit sweater were exchanged for smooth, soft cut-offs that owed their luster and pale blue color to innumerable washings, and a khaki T-shirt with green lettering that read M A S H. Time was taken to devour a tuna sandwich and check what was available for dinner. Amanda decided to serve the individual frozen quiches with a salad—after all, she had a lot of walls to stucco!

The newly acquired foliage was given a hose shower and left in the courtyard to enjoy the sunlight. By midafternoon, five gallons of parchment paint had been applied to the living-room walls with a deep textured roller that gave a heavy stippling stucco effect.

Amanda was trying to decide whether to open gallon

number six when Lucas came whistling through the front doorway. "Watch your step," she cautioned, wiping her hands on the seat of her ragged-edged shorts. "I didn't expect you for another two hours."

"My court case was postponed until tomorrow, and my calendar was empty, so . . ." His voice trailed off once his eyes discovered the extent of her labors. Lucas swallowed. "I . . . I can't believe you've got this much done. It looks great!"

Amanda blew on her paint-crusted fingernails, polishing the roughness on her cotton shirt. "Thank you, kind sir." She walked toward him, bare feet pulling free of the plastic drop cloth. "Hmm. I really do believe this little gadget works!" She pretended fascination with a small object cupped in her palm.

"What have you got there?" Lucas pulled off his black and red striped tie, tossing it over his arm on top of his folded charcoal suit jacket.

"The man at the hardware store said I couldn't hang plants without toggle bolts, and I couldn't sink a toggle bolt into a beam unless I had"—her toes overlapped his shoetips, her gray eyes sparkled with coquettish mockery—"a stud finder." Her laughter flirted. "I see it works on nonwooden studs."

His teeth flashed with wolfish intent. "You got taken, kid. All you have to do is thump to find the studs."

Amanda's knuckles gave a suggestive rap against Lucas' shoulder. "I'll let you do the thumping," came her sassy rejoinder. "Go change and grab that stepladder, there's—"

"I know, I saw the jungle out front." Lucas held his thumbs up for her inspection. "Do these look green to you?"

She gently twisted his proffered digits in the direction of his bedroom and pointedly ignored his grumbled complaints by heading outside to start transplanting.

The vivid air had been replaced by a heavy, humid blanket. Brooding clouds banded together, growling and chasing the afternoon sun from the sky. But the dismal, slanting rain had little effect on the garden that was being created inside the triple arched windows.

"I think we should give each plant a name." Amanda settled in a comfortable Indian-style position amid the empty remains of their indoor picnic.

Lucas looked up from refilling their glasses with icy white Chablis. "I don't know, Mandy, a name, that's so personal." He squinted at the windows, the foliage drapes illuminated by a reading lamp brought in to provide working light. "I'm going to feel guilty when they shrivel up and end up buried in the mulch pit."

A feminine hand slapped his denim-covered thigh. "These plants are virtually impossible to kill, Lucas."

Amanda's fingernail scratched off a patch of paint that a soapy washcloth and a hot shower had failed to dissolve. "I think we'll call the ficus tree Perry Mason, since he holds court in the center; the coleus will be Della Street, because she'll need an occasional pinch; that spider plant is a perfect representative for that long arm of the law, Lieutenant Tragg; the assorted ivies will be Paul Drake's detectives; and that pompous-looking fern will be the never-winning DA, Hamilton Burger."

Applause and laughter accompanied each of her suggestions. Lucas wiped his eyes and cleared his throat. "Erle Stanley Gardner is probably rolling over in his grave. Mandy, how the hell do you know all those fictional characters?"

Avoiding his inquiring gaze, she concentrated on the tan top-stitching that decorated the patch pockets on her olive twill pants. "I read every Perry Mason mystery from the *Case of the Velvet Claws* to the *Case of the Postponed Murder* while you were in law school." Amanda bolstered herself with sips of wine as she made her confession.

"I remember thinking at the time, reading Gardner would be the quickest way for me to learn a modicum of law without being bored and perhaps dazzle you with something legally profound. The author was a skilled lawyer, so I knew the facts in the books would be correct even though the stories were fiction." A half smile quirked her lips. "I always had this . . . this silly dream that one day you'd turn into a lawyer-detective à la Perry Mason."

Lucas gave a rueful laugh. "The only time I get to play detective is when I hunt for precedents." Rolling on his side, his long fingers walked the few inches needed to curve around her wrist. "That was really a wonderful thing for you to do, Mandy." His deep voice held no hint of teasing.

"I always liked being able to share in what you were studying, Lucas. I knew I'd drive you crazy with questions, so . . ."

"Actually," his thumb and forefinger smoothed his dark moustache, "I have a confession to make." At her inquiring arched brow, Lucas gave a self-conscious laugh. "I used to read all those *Women's Wear Daily*'s you tossed out so I wouldn't make any fashion *faux pas* and say that Coco Chanel was a type of French hot chocolate."

Amanda leaned from the waist, her lips a breath away from his firmly molded mouth. "She was, Lucas." Her fingers caressed the white collar and placket on his burgundy sport shirt. "Very French, very hot and"—the pupils of her eyes glittered like onyx rimmed with silver—"just as consuming a passion as choc-o-late." She was flirting again—but neither of them seemed to mind.

"I'm buying you a housewarming present," Amanda announced at breakfast.

Lucas looked over the top of the sports section. "Don't be silly! All the decorating you're doing is certainly present enough." He refilled his empty mug from the percolator sitting on the kitchen counter.

"No. No. I really want to. I insist."

"Okay."

She laughed and shook her head. "You're such a hard sell, Lucas!"

"Hey, I know better than to argue with you." He confiscated the last piece of toast. "What am I going to be getting?"

Amanda tapped the newspaper. "Neiman's January in

April white sale starts tomorrow. Since you're taking me into Dallas, I can stop and get you new bath towels." She sipped her coffee. "Listen to these colors: cantaloupe, peach, cinnamon, nutmeg."

"Sounds a little too fruity and spicy for me." Lucas' words were mumbled around buttered bread.

"Listen," she pulled down the newspaper, "as a guest, your towels leave a lot to be desired. You've got"—Amanda held up her hand, her fingers ticking off each statement—"five from various hotels, four from NYU, three from the health club, two from the U.S. Army and—"

"A partridge in a pear tree?" His hazel eyes were alive with laughter.

She gave an unladylike snort. "Believe me, Lucas, I don't think any bird would consider nesting in one of your towels."

"Okay, okay," his hands were held in a gesture of surrender, "Just buy more spice than fruits." The digital display on his watch snagged his attention. "I've got to run. It's going to be all day in court for me." Lucas slid off the barstool and reached for the raw silk jacket that matched his taupe slacks.

"I'm going to phone in a wallpaper order. I found the perfect pattern for the kitchen and one for the foyer in those sample books I prowled through last night." Amanda twisted around in the swivel seat, reaching up to straighten the lopsided knot in his gold and black striped tie. "You look very nice." She patted the light blue shirt collar.

His nose wrinkled at her paint-spattered work clothes. "Well, despite your tawdry attire, Miss Wyatt"—bending his head, Lucas rested his forehead against hers—"it's certainly wonderful to see your beautiful face over the newspaper in the morning." He had meant to kiss her nose but somehow his mouth found it impossible to ignore the silent invitation of her lips.

Amanda ordered a flame-stitch, earth-toned fabric for the entry hall and a leather look-alike in bronze for the kitchen. She was promised delivery early on Friday along with the appropriate hanging tools and paste.

Intricate plots and characters on the daytime soap operas kept her company while she sculpted stucco swirls on the last two walls and made necessary touch-ups. The couple on TV were enjoying a romantic interlude on a sunny Caribbean island (totally ignorant of the evil being plotted against them) when Amanda rudely became aware that she too was being threatened.

The sunlight illuminating her work area was rapidly dissipating, and by four o'clock the clear, azure Texas sky resembled midnight. Rain had yet to make an appearance, but thunder and lightning heralded its iminent arrival.

Lucas, however, proved more turbulent than the forthcoming storm. His raging masculine bellow caused Amanda to drop her trowel. "What the—"

An upraised hand halted her question, even more so than the violent expression that contorted his normally placid features. Lucas marched through the house and through the patio doorway, jacket and tie thrown in his wake.

Amanda gave an expressive shrug, wiped her hands on a cloth and followed. She found him at the woodpile, yanking an ax from a tree stump.

"You lost the case."

"I did *not* lose the case." He placed a log on the stump, motioned for her to step back, then heaved the ax. The wood was split neatly in two.

"You had an accident."

"I did *not* have an accident." Another limb shattered under the guillotine blade, the dry wood crackling louder than the lightning.

"You got a ticket."

"I did *not* get a ticket." Lucas cleared his throat, wiping his sweat-beaded forehead on his shirt sleeve. "I have a headache."

Amanda's mouth twisted in a grimace, her right foot burrowed into the dirt. "I didn't know chopping wood was more effective than aspirin."

Three more boughs were lacerated. "Aspirin," he took two deep steadying breaths, his massive chest heaving under inner tensions, "aspirin will not cure this headache. A drink will not cure this headache." Lucas grabbed another log. "Destroying something . . . *that* will cure this headache."

A large drop of rain splashed Amanda's arm. Her face turned upward, more droplets pelted her cheek and nose. "Why don't I get cleaned up and start dinner." She reached for a few pieces of the already stacked firewood. "Whenever you finish destroying your quota," she said, shivering against another wet assault, "why don't you come in and we can talk."

The slate hearth was set in lieu of a table. Pristine white plates, polished silverware and two crystal goblets waited impatiently to hold a banquet of roasted hot dogs, German potato salad and "long necks"—Lone Star's finest brew.

A sheepish Lucas knelt on the floor cushion, his dark gaze focused on the warm, steady flame that crackled in a friendly greeting.

"Mustard, relish and onions. One perfectly accessorized frankfurter." Amanda placed the bun-wrapped entrée on his plate. "Are you feeling any better?"

"Un-huh." He shook a bottle free of the ice-packed spittoon, twisted the cap and poured two glasses of beer, the foam a perfect half-inch head on the golden, effervescent liquid.

Amanda sighed and complacently chewed her dinner. "Of course, you do realize you're going to be arrested for murder."

His dark brows pulled together in silent confusion.

"I'm dying of curiosity." She wiped her mouth on a napkin, her words exhaled in a rush. "You chopped enough wood for two winters, then you were in the shower for twenty minutes, took your sweet time changing into a sweat shirt and jeans and now"—Amanda's hands cradled Lucas' face—"you're sitting here not saying a word." Her fingers rubbed against the stubble on his jaw. "Lucas, you know I hate the strong, silent type!"

Two heavy masculine arms were draped around her neck. Lucas rested his chin on Amanda's soft, terrycovered shoulder. "I had a terrible day, Mandy." He groaned in her ear, taking a deep breath. The clean soapscent of her skin excited his nostrils. His hands roamed freely over her back, fingers making random zigzags in the blue material. "I wished the courtroom floor had opened up and swallowed me, but it didn't."

"Poor baby." Amanda wrapped her arms around him, hugging Lucas as if he were a small child. "What happened?"

"This was the most idiotic insurance case I've ever handled. The people were con artists, the claim was a fraud and their attorney is one of the city's best-known shysters."

"But Lucas, you said you didn't lose the case."

"I know. I didn't. I won."

"Lucas." Amanda's voice lowered in a distinct threat, her fingers giving a light tug against the thick hair that curled on the nape. "What happened?"

Another groan was issued. "I had just finished punching holes in the so-called eyewitness's testimony when the aforementioned lady witness said to the judge"—Lucas' deep voice rose three octaves—"Your Honor, that attorney's so cute. I want to know if he'll go out with me tonight."

Amanda coughed, cleared her throat but couldn't contain the hysterical bubble that finally erupted. She collapsed backward on the floor, hands trying to ward off Lucas' irate strangler attack. "I'm sorry. Really . . ." she sniffed and blinked. "That's why you were so upset, because she called you cute?"

"Damn it, Mandy, of course I was upset." Disgusted with her reaction, he turned back to his dinner. "I did not appreciate being called *cute* when I was trying to be tough and uncompromising." He drained his glass, hoping the cold beer would temper his anger. "The courtroom broke up, and so did Judge Hollander. I was demoralized." Another beer cap was twisted.

"Lucas." Amanda scrambled on her knees to his side. Her hand caught his face, thumb and pinky finding the dimpled indentations in his cheeks. "You are cute."

Lucas pulled away. "Amanda, *cute* is fine when you're three," his tone curt and cold.

She cleared her throat and sighed. "You're absolutely right." Her fingernail lightly scratched a jagged line from his eye to the corner of his frowning mouth. "How about a scar?" Her laughing suggestion was rewarded by a hot dog stuffed between her lips.

The brown Fiat turned past the Quadrangle Shopping Center and headed for Cedar Springs. "I really love this part of the city," Lucas told Amanda. "The homes have been converted to offices, restaurants and boutiques. It's very"—he searched for the correct adjective—"quaint and relaxed, more so than the glass-and-steel edifices downtown."

Amanda's gray eyes studied his rugged profile. "Just as long as no one describes the area as cute." Her smile belied her grave tone.

He reached over and rearranged her sienna curls. "That's enough, Mandy," came his gruff warning. "You teased me enough last night."

"Did I ever tell you that my mother's initial reaction to you was—"

"If you value your life, don't say—"

"Cute!" The word was spoken in unison. The tiny car echoed with shared laughter.

"This *is* charming," Amanda agreed as the Fiat was parked in front of a post-World War II-style bungalow. The gabled roof and porch stood white against deep red aluminum siding.

At the front door, she paused to let her fingertips trace the engraved letters on the shingle that proclaimed: LUCAS CROSSE, ATTORNEY-AT-LAW. "I can't believe you still have this." Amanda shook her head in amazement. "I gave that to you—"

"Nine years ago," Lucas supplied. His hand slid around

her neck. "I packed that sign away with inordinate care. I knew someday it would grace my own office."

The reception area was attractive and functional in design. The black and pewter tweed carpet emphasized the monochromatic color scheme. Smart, polished chrome sled-base chairs, with black upholstered arms and seats, formed dual modular groupings that were serviced by glass and chrome end tables. Crisp white plaster walls displayed large photographs that depicted old and new Dallas in historical daguerreotypes.

"The building rented furnished; fortunately my office isn't quite this modern," Lucas explained, hanging Amanda's desert-hued striped jacket on the valet rack. "I share half the building with Gary LaBelle. He's a C.P.A. and we often give each other clients."

An interior door swung open. A jovial, thinly lined feminine face framed by close-cropped black hair peered out. "Good morning, Mr. Crosse. I though I heard someone out here."

"Gloria Dale, meet Amanda Wyatt." Lucas' broad smile encompassed both women. "Gloria keeps both offices running smoothly. She's our resident wizard."

"That nifty little word processor you and Gary bought, that's what makes me a wizard." Gloria moved behind her desk, settling her bifocals into position. Dark brown eyes assessed Amanda's jade blouse and burlap brown bias skirt that was casually elegant compared to her own austere gray flannel suit.

Gloria snapped her finger. "You're the fashion designer Lucas always talks about. Maybe we could have a chat." Her dark head nodded toward her boss. "Lucas and Gary call me the 'gray lady.' " Her fingers ran up and down the lapels on her jacket. "But in my day this was the office uniform."

"And still very attractive," Amanda complimented with a smile. "That suit emphasizes your slender figure perfectly."

"Why . . . why, thank you." The other woman's cheeks took on a petal pink glow. "You know, my daughters are always teasing me to 'get with it.' " Gloria's expression turned serious. "Do you think at fifty-six I'm too old to make a few costume changes?"

"Women don't get older, we get better." Amanda favored her with an outrageous wink. "I'll be glad to rough out a few fashion ideas to update your gray flannel wardrobe if you'd like."

"I'd love it!" Gloria cleared her throat and suddenly became all business. "Now then, Lucas," she opened a file folder and began to sift through various pink-slipped messages, "I expected you to call in yesterday after court. Your whole day has been restructured."

"Oh, no." He looked toward Amanda, a frown etching his lips.

"Court has been changed to a meeting in Judge Reinhardt's chambers at ten. You've got two afternoon appointments: one at two and one at four."

"Don't worry about me," Amanda said, patting her taupe leather shoulder bag. "I'm headed for Neiman's and then furniture hunting."

"You might want to explore these furniture warehouses." Gloria jotted two notations on a slip of paper and handed it to Amanda. "Both have excellent merchandise at discount prices."

Lucas gathered up the morning mail. "I guess you have enough shopping to keep you occupied, Mandy, but I really wanted you to spend a day with me in court." His long legs quickly covered the short distance to his office.

"We can plan it for another day, Lucas." Her amiable tone strove to soothe his ruffled ego. "Now, this . . . this is you," Amanda announced, surveying the stylish wood executive office.

The atmosphere was relaxed but impressive. Caramel walls and mahogany brown carpet were tranquil to the senses. The large walnut desk was flanked by a rust upholstered executive chair and two matching captain-style guest chairs. Bookcases formed a ninety-degree angle filled with legal information. The opposite wall was balanced by a walnut credenza over which framed university and law school degrees hung in imposing silence.

Placing his leather attaché case on the desk, Lucas came to Amanda's side, hands moving along the slender length of her arms. "Do you really like it?"

Her head tilted back, and the soft copper curls caressed the shoulder of his navy blazer. "I love it. This room reflects its owner. Confident, judicious, tough, secure." Her next words were whispered impishly into her ear. "All you need is a bust of Blackstone. Hmm . . . maybe I'll add that to my shopping list."

While Neiman-Marcus offered a chocolate Monopoly set, they did not possess a sculpture of the famous English jurist, Sir William Blackstone. That fact did not deter Amanda from inspecting every inch of the seven floors and wishing the other two under construction were finished. She purchased six complete towel ensembles, two in pale pastels, the others in Lucas' requested *macho* spice.

Gloria's suggestion to scout furniture warehouses proved lucrative to both Amanda and the bespectacled salesman who dogged her every step. The store provided quality, variety and quick availability.

A very attractive living-room suite was displayed in the window. While the textured diamond design was cream in color, the fabric had Scotchguard and was sturdy, the natural wood trim in excellent agreement with the architectural beams in Lucas' living room. The portly, attentive salesman eagerly wrote a purchase order for a sofa, love seat, side chair and ottoman, matching recliner, three end tables and a coffee table. Amanda was given an extra discount for cash, and delivery was promised for the next day.

The second store was having a bankruptcy sale. Among the odds and ends, Amanda bought three brass-based lamps, a light oak wall unit and a dresser with a mirror that would be useful in the guest bedroom. At the adjoining rug outlet, two matching oriental look-alikes were added. The Tree of Life pattern was done in rust, brown, beige and gray, coordinating perfectly with the furniture and the teak flooring.

It was nearly five when Amanda stumbled into the air-conditioned comfort of Lucas' law office. With a wan smile at Gloria, Amanda sank into a chair, eased off her vanilla pumps and flexed her cramped fingers.

"It looks like you had a successful day." Gloria administered some thirst-quenching first aid in the form of iced tea. "Lucas is on the phone long distance. His last appointment just left."

Amanda savored the refreshing drink. "Thank you." She lifted the glass in an appreciative gesture. "By the way, I found some fashion magazines for the working woman that might interest you." She hunted through numerous colored shopping bags, not finding the right one until the last try. "Also, Neiman's has a wardrobe counseling service; the lady to call is Helen Stevens. Here's her card, and here are four tickets to a fashion show they're having next month." Gloria was presented with an ever growing stack of information. "I didn't know how many daughters you had. I hope those will be enough."

"This is marvelous." The secretary clutched the material against her chest. "I have two daughters and a niece who are going to be thrilled. Amanda, this was so nice of you. How did you manage? Tickets to a Neiman's fashion show are like gold!"

Smiling, Amanda looked up from massaging her stocking-clad foot. "I just happened to run into their buyer, whom I had met in New York a couple of years ago. We had a catch-up chat over lunch and . . ." She sighed and leaned back in her chair. "Listen, I can't thank you enough for the tip on the furniture stores. Lucas' new living room will be arriving tomorrow."

"Does this mean my bank balance is zero?" Lucas' deep voice intoned from the open doorway.

"Actually, I still have quite a ways to go before it's depleted." Amanda's smile turned serious. "I think you'll be pleased with everything, Lucas. The furniture is comfortable and casual but has that"—she kissed her fingers, her eyes sassy—"touch of class you requested."

Laughing, he moved to her side. His strong hands administered a gentle massage to her tired shoulder muscles. "You look like you could use a drink and a good dinner." Hazel eyes radiated concern.

"Just as long as I don't have to make either of the above." Her words were punctuated by a series of yawns.

The Antare's provided two perfectly dry martinis with a twist and a gourmet dinner menu. The elegant, slowly rotating restaurant sat atop the landmark fifty-story Reunion Tower, glass windows giving patrons a breathtaking view of Dallas.

"I have some good news and some bad news," Lucas informed Amanda after placing an order for two rare slabs of prime Texas beef with all the trimmings. "I have to fly to El Paso on business tomorrow, and it means I'll be gone overnight."

"Now, what's the bad news?" she teased, reaching for the last stuffed mushroom.

Lucas confiscated her forked hors d'oeuvre, savoring the buttery crab filling in his own mouth. "The good news," he continued, ignoring her contrived pout, "is that Kitty called and told me her party is set for Friday night."

"Sounds good." Amanda removed her elbows from the table, allowing the waiter room to serve the salad. "I've been feeling very guilty, Lucas. You've been home with me every night. I don't want you to ignore Kitty."

He hesitated slightly, his fork toying with a sliced cucumber. "Kitty has been tied up with a big real-estate deal she's been putting together." Lucas chose his words carefully. "Our relationship isn't one that demands daily contact."

"Intimate but informal," she suggested, selecting a warm muffin over the traditional dinner rolls.

"You could say that." Adroitly, he changed the subject. "Why was it you insisted on carrying this," the toe of his brown leather shoe tapped the neatly wrapped package, "up here?"

"Hey, watch it." Amanda carefully inspected the parcel that had been wedged underneath their table. "This is a work of art."

"Show me."

The wrapping paper was removed to display an unframed canvas. An artist's creative touch with oil had reproduced a French street scene—sidewalk café, flower cart and strolling tourists.

"I just couldn't resist it." Amanda wrinkled her nose at Lucas. "Call me a sentimentalist."

He appeared hurt. "You mean it's not for me?"

"Lucas," she looked up in surprise, "this wouldn't suit you at all. Maybe something in a southwestern motif, or perhaps a three-dimensional fresco."

"But I like this painting." He laid a possessive hand on the canvas.

"Now, wait just a minute." Her fingers curved around the opposite corner. "Lucas, this is silly."

"What's so silly?" His tone was quite serious. "I happen to like . . . no . . . *love* this painting. Look at those colors: rich, vivid, refreshing. The brushstrokes are bold but balanced." With his free hand, Lucas reached inside his jacket pocket, searching for his checkbook. "I'll buy it from you."

Amanda took a deep breath. "It's not for sale."

"How about half?" Lucas knew he was babbling nonsense, but somehow the painting represented more than a work of art—it was another bond. "I could write out a joint-custody plan. We both could have visitation rights. Six months with you; six months with me."

She looked startled, then laughed. "Lucas, you are crazy!" Amanda rewrapped the painting and put it safely between her legs. "If you're very nice to me," dark lashes fluttered like black lace against her cheeks, "I might let you have it during the holidays."

Buttercup and Maizey were to be fed twice a day and brushed down at night. Amanda added a lunchtime treat of apples and carrots to her stalwart companions' menu.

The furniture arrived just as promised, but not in the correct order—the rugs arrived last. The two deliverymen were more than happy to move the heavy items to allow the laying of the carpet; their kind efforts were rewarded with cold lemonade and homebaked brownies.

Amanda was enormously pleased with her selections. The sofa and love seat formed a warm conversational group in the main living area, the oak wall unit balanced the fireplace and stood waiting to accommodate Lucas' stereo and TV, the double-door cabinet would serve as a bar.

The chair, ottoman and matching recliner were well proportioned for the alcove, with room still available for a desk. Here was the perfect spot to sit and read in front of a blazing fire on a stormy night.

Despite the fact it was another cloudy day and rain-swept night, Amanda pushed aside the thought of a cozy fire and a good book and turned instead to her decorating. The kitchen and entry foyer walls were sized for subsequent wallpapering, and Lucas' bedroom received a primer coat in anticipation of the real thing, which was on the schedule for the next day.

It was nearly midnight when the telephone extended a cordial beep. "Hi, Mandy. How's everything going?" Lucas' deep voice inquired.

"Just fine. The furniture arrived. I can't wait for you to see it."

"I wish I were there. It's hot and muggy here."

"It's like that where I am." Amanda's throaty laughter drifted through the lines. "I'm glad you put a long extension cord on the telephone, Lucas. It makes taking a bath a pleasure. You don't have to drip all over when someone calls."

"So you're enjoying my sunken tub, are you?"

"Very much." Her voice was as sultry as the temperature in the room. "How did your meeting go?"

"Excellent. I have a new client."

"Congratulations!" Her voice reflected more than enthusiasm. "Lucas, I'm so proud of you. Your business is growing every day."

"I like having you as my cheerleader," came his teasing rejoinder. "Listen, Mandy, I'm going to have to stay for meetings tomorrow, so I won't be home until six."

"That's okay. I'm painting your bedroom. I found a terrific shade called morning glory; it seems to change with the light."

"You could take a day off," Lucas suggested. "You're doing more work now than I ever intended. This was supposed to be a vacation," came his gentle reminder.

"I really am having fun. I'm enjoying every minute of this." Amanda took a deep breath before asking the one question that had been on her mind. "Lucas, if there's anything you don't like . . . please tell me. This is *your* house."

"But it's taken you to turn it into a home."

"Mandy, I'm . . . I'm . . ." Lucas' voice sputtered in dumbfounded amazement. "Mandy, you are too much," came his whispered words of praise. The new living room glowed under soft lights. He fingered a parchment shade on the hexagonal brass table lamp, then let his hand stroke the nubby-textured sofa upholstery. "Mandy?"

"I'm in your room," she caroled. "How was your flight?"

"Delayed." He headed down the hallway backward, his eyes still inspecting the luxurious new furnishings. "I hope you're ready. Kitty's party starts in fifteen minutes, so we're already late. I just want to change my—"

A low groan escaped Amanda, roller in hand. She looked down at her paint-spattered, sweaty anatomy. "Lucas . . ." Her wide-eyed face greeted him. "I . . . I forgot. I got so involved. These darn walls just soaked up this paint, and I wanted the room finished tonight. I'm sorry."

"Amanda!"

"Okay, don't panic. No problem." She put down the roller and wiped off her hands. "Just give me a minute to clean this mess up. I'll grab a shower, use the blower on my hair. I promise I won't embarrass you."

"You never embarrass me, Mandy." His hands curled

around her paint-spangled forearms, his face etched with tender regard. "Amaze me, always."

Twenty minutes later, Lucas ventured a knock on Amanda's partially open door. "How are you doing?"

"Not bad. Come on in. I'm putting on my makeup." She peered at her reflection using a cotton swab to smudge kohl shadow on her eyelids. "Did Kitty say how populated and formal this gathering is going to be?" His suit-clad image loomed large in the mirror.

"I think it's going to be slightly more formal than this peach towel you're wrapped in." Lucas grinned, and his masculine gaze languorously viewed her scantily clad curves.

"Well," Amanda paused to add a coat of mascara to her lashes, "everyone gets to see my 'drop dead' dress for this year." Her eyebrows arched suggestively, her thumb gestured toward the closet. "Can you get my low-heeled black dress sandals?"

"Here you go." The grooves in Lucas' cheeks deepened with amusement as he stared at her feet. "Mandy, I think you missed with the soap."

She looked down. Paint covered toenails wiggled against the wood floor. "Damn, I was in such a rush and they'll show! Oh, Lucas, I need an extra pair of hands."

"You've got them." He picked up a bottle of nail polish remover from the dresser. "Where's some cotton?" he shook the pale green liquid. "You keep working on the top half, I'll do the bottom." With unaccustomed delicacy, Lucas removed the final traces of paint, then added poppy red polish to Amanda's splayed toes.

Capping the bottle, he surveyed his artistic endeavor. "Not too shabby. What do you think, Mandy?" His voice raised over the wail of the hair dryer.

She switched off the blower, her fingers fluffing through disarrayed curls. "You make a perfect lady's maid, Lucas." Her gray eyes glittered with rascally delight. "Now scat so I can throw my dress on and we can make a grand entrance!"

Chapter Six

"Is MY LIPSTICK crooked?" Amanda turned her face toward Lucas, letting the mirror in her compact aid in reflecting the elevator's subdued light.

He dutifully inspected perfectly coated mauve lips. "You look like you've spent the day at the beauty shop." Lucas continued to stare, wondering how Amanda had ever made such a stunning transformation. She looked vibrant and relaxed; there was no hint that she had been costumed in paint forty minutes ago.

When the deep purple evening shawl slipped off Amanda's shoulders, Lucas' eyebrow lifted at his first glimpse of her attire. "I think, however," he found his tone quite cool, "that you missed getting your dress on straight."

She gazed down at the adventurous red lace-up bodice that was sashed in hot pink, with a tiered skirt in deep purple, hot pink and red. "No, it's just fine." Amanda pointedly ignored his comment. Her fingers moved from her collarbone along a creamy expanse of naked shoulders to the red lace bow that suggestively delineated the valley between her full breasts.

"I thought you would have worn something . . . something . . ." His thoughts failing him, Lucas concentrated on the toes of his brown leather shoes.

"Something black with a high neck and covered to the ankles," Amanda's lilting voice filled in the blanks. "Really, Lucas, I'm sure everyone expects me to provide a little panache, an ensemble with a little spark, a little zip."

Lucas sucked in his cheeks. "You've done well. The

problem is, the dress provides too little coverage for your zips!"

She laughed, her elbow nudging his arm. "Lucas, don't be such a prude."

He grunted and when the elevator doors opened, long legs stalked down the thickly carpeted corridor to Kitty's apartment.

"Luke!" A petite blond bundle catapulted into his arms. "I thought you had stood me up."

Amanda's eyes widened slightly at the diminutive given Lucas' name; he had once told her he hated the nickname Luke.

"Just running a little late." Unhooking her hands from around his neck, Lucas readjusted the collar of his beige shirt and smoothed his brown tie. "Kitty Byrnes, meet Amanda Wyatt."

Kitty's blue gaze had already looked beyond his shoulder, femininely sizing up an unknown quantity. She extended her hand. "Luke makes you sound so perfect I almost dreaded meeting you."

Amanda smiled. "He speaks the same way about you. I'm glad we're able to get together."

Kitty stood to one side as they entered the small foyer. "One of the first things I noticed about Luke was his clothes." Her hand possessively settled on Lucas' sleeve, fingers luxuriating against the expensive brown tickweave. "I can thank you for that.

"I think that old adage is true that clothes make the man or the woman." Kitty's slim jeweled fingers picked an infinitesimal thread from the strapless royal purple bodice of her dress, then moved down to straighten her marigold bubble knee-length skirt. She felt a desperate need to show off the Bob Evans designer label. "But I guess that's the first thing you notice being in the fashion industry. You must continually size up people by their clothing."

"Actually, I've always looked first in a person's eyes." Amanda's tone was warm and friendly. "Eyes are the mirrors of the soul." She looked at Lucas, and a soft smile curved her lips. "Lucas' hazel eyes were very kind and patient. I'm afraid I've taken advantage of him over the years."

He caught her wrist, the wide gold bracelet cool beneath his hand. "I've had numerous fringe benefits," came his grinning quip.

Kitty looked from one to the other, still puzzled and uncertain about this relationship. "Come on, Amanda, let me introduce you. Luke, I think you know just about everyone. Why don't you get some drinks."

The cocktail party had reached its peak, conversations were shrill, gestures had broadened expansively, the music was a shade too loud. Amanda put an "I'm so thrilled to meet you" smile on and made appropriate small talk to all those who were presented. Kitty was an attentive hostess, leaving her side only when another guest gave an emergency bellow.

Lucas, Amanda observed, had been cornered by a man introduced as another lawyer and appeared deep in conversation. She took her brief respite from inane chitchat to appreciate Kitty's apartment. The living-dining room was spacious and originally decorated in a plum and gold color scheme that complemented the sophisticated furnishings. She wondered why Lucas hadn't asked Kitty for input into his house.

Amanda's attention was focused on one of the many abstract paintings that accessorized the contemporary theme, trying to interpret whether a series of three-dimensional purple and gold hexagonal cubes were being thrust inward (pessimist) or outward (optimist) when an unfamiliar male voice spoke in her ear.

"I've been trying to decide if you're white wine or brandy."

Her head tilted sideways, gray eyes locked into bright blue irises. "And what have you decided?"

"That it's a shame a drink can't be invented to accommodate them both." His attractive, weathered face held an engaging smile. "I think you're crisp and assertive as well as mellow and potent. Tonight, however, you're quite intoxicating and that's why . . ." He gifted her with a balloon snifter.

When their fingers touched, he added, "I'm Wade Lloyd. I apologize for missing your introduction."

"Amanda Wyatt," she supplied. Her mind registered thick, straight hair that was more silver than black despite the fact that Wade appeared to be about the same age as Lucas. His height was on a par with her own; his broad shoulders and well-proportioned body were emphasized by an expertly tailored gray pinstriped suit.

"I've heard a lot about you from Kitty." At her silent inquiry Wade smiled and explained. "Kitty works in my real-estate office. So naturally"—his glass-laden hand made an expressive gesture—"your name has been mentioned in connection with Lucas." His eyes scanned the velvet skin exposed by the torso-hugging camisole. "I find I'm quite envious of Crosse's relationship."

Diamond-bright eyes sparkled with flirty delight. "And don't you have," Amanda paused to sip the aged cognac, "an enviable relationship?"

Wade's fingers moved to straighten the coin-littered gold necklace that caressed her throat. "No relationships whatsoever." His deep voice issued an obvious but pleasing invitation.

"That doesn't say much for the Dallas ladies," she bantered. Amanda was enjoying herself, playing the "man-woman" teasing game; it had been a long time. She suddenly felt revitalized.

His glass lifted to his lips. "Maybe I'll find a Louisiana woman more to my liking." Wade's hand cupped her elbow, guiding her to an unoccupied plum velvet two-seat modular grouping at the very edge of the laughing, chattering crowd.

Placing her glass on the round coffee table, Amanda gave Wade her full attention. The soft light cast deliciously dangerous shadows. Her sleek, suggestive piratical outfit duplicated the boldness of her manner. "I'm interested to know what differences you discover."

"I'm positive my investigation will take more time than

tonight." His head nodded toward Lucas, who was in conversation with Kitty. "Would there be a problem if I call you?"

Her husky laugh sought to dispel any doubts. "You seem to find it difficult to believe that Lucas and I have a close and platonic friendship."

Even white teeth flashed. "Platonic . . . that's what *I* would have trouble with." His head leaned toward her. "The two of you, all alone, all night . . ." Wade's voice trailed off suggestively.

Dark lashes fluttered, mauve lips formed a childlike pout. "I've been nothing but the soul of discretion." Amanda gave an exaggerated sigh. "It has been something of a strain." Her outrageous wink brought forth dual laughter.

"And what has Crosse been doing to keep you busy?" Wade relaxed into the confines of the chair, his fingers casually brushing the lush material of her skirt.

Pretense and teasing were put aside, and Amanda was once again herself. "Lucas invited me for a vacation and to help him decorate his remodeled house." She smiled. "It's been fun. I've stuccoed walls, painted and papered, ordered furniture . . ."

"Hmmm," he captured her hand, "all that and they're soft as silk."

"An hour ago they were covered in latex morning glory." Khol-shadowed lids lowered, Amanda shivered slightly as Wade traced each poppy-enameled finger, then zigzagged an erotic pattern against her palm.

"How long is your vacation?"

"I have no time limit." Her body edged forward, eyes flecked with silver fire. She was finding Wade more attractive and intriguing with each passing minute, and by all indications those feelings were reciprocated.

He smiled slightly; the creases deepened in his cheeks. "I seem to remember Kitty telling me that you own a . . . dress shop in the French Quarter."

"Rags 'n' Riches," Amanda supplied. "It's more than a *dress shop.*" Her tone was light but there was a subtle bit of censure. "We're well known in this country and on the Continent for offering the ultimate in fashion."

"I'm afraid I know little about the world of high fashion," Wade apologized. His blue eyes journeyed over her eloquent attire. "But I do know what I like, and if that charming creation is from your boutique . . ."

She nodded. "Not only from my shop but also from my design board."

He toasted her with his glass. "A woman of many talents."

Amanda's hand reached out to straighten the gold initial tack that held his black pindotted silk tie. "And what of your talents, Wade?" She hesitated slightly. "I understand your real-estate business is booming."

"Texas is certainly the place to sell land," he agreed. "I've been very lucky this year. I hope it continues."

"What is the big attraction?" she persisted, liking the melodic timbre of his voice. "Housing, office complexes, industrial plants?"

"Pick one." Wade laughed, and his silver head gave a curious shake. "Real estate is an ambiguous field, Amanda. Interest rates are sky high but, here at least, there are developers willing to invest in the future. Right now big business seems to be moving to the Sun Belt, and Texas is very attractive, lots of land, no state income tax, good work force."

"How did you happen to become a broker?"

Wade cleared his throat and rubbed his jaw. "You're looking at a former systems analyst." He gave her a crooked smile. "When the space program was cut in '69, I singlehandedly saved the economy by going off unemployment and getting into real estate." His bright eyes were laughing. "I was twenty-six and very cocky. I remember sitting with my calculator figuring out my commission on all these multimillion-dollar transactions I was planning."

Amanda found his honesty appealing and his story fascinating. She coaxed Wade to continue. His low, vibrant voice stirred her senses. Her eyes savored his features—the shaggy haircut that looked well groomed but not too

perfect; firm chin and rugged jawline; well-shaped ear-
lobes; the small mole by his sideburns; and above all, the
laugh lines deeply etched around his blue eyes.

Above all, she liked the excitement he fed into the conversation. Amanda was made to feel as if she had been
there, with him, every step of the way. Wade enjoyed making life an adventure, and she found that stimulating. Her
own energy source seemed to be refueling and so did the
hidden fires that had been dormant for so long.

Wade drew a deep breath, interrupting his own mono-
logue. "Damn, I can't believe I've been going on like this.
Amanda, I apologize." He uncomfortably rubbed the back
of his neck. "There's nothing more boring than being regaled with a stranger's life story." He reached for his
drink, trying to ease his discomfort.

"I can't believe that I've just admitted getting a rash
from tomatoes and preferring Chinese food over Texas
beef. You must have been bored. I—"

Amanda's hand gently stilled his lips. "Not bored. Fascinated."

His cobalt gaze focused on her mouth. "That makes two
of us." Wade leaned closer, his hand trailed the length of
her slender arm to her collarbone. "Amanda, why don't we
make our escape and—"

"This is quite a coup." Kitty's slightly shrill voice invaded their intimate tête-à-tête. "Usually my anti-party
boss is the first one to leave. Tonight he's the last."

Both Amanda and Wade cast a surprised glance around
the empty, well-littered room. "This was one of your better
get-togethers, Kitty," came Wade's wry comment. He
stood to shake hands with Lucas. "Nice to see you again.
You have excellent taste in friends."

Lucas cast a jaundiced eye at Amanda's glowing face.
"I've always thought so." He settled his tall frame in the
adjoining modular two-seat unit.

Amanda shifted uncomfortably in the ensuing silence.
"Kitty, why don't I help you clean up." She smiled the offer. "There's nothing worse than waking up the morning
after to face the night before."

Kitty gave a dismissing gesture, collapsing next to Lucas. "Someone's coming in tomorrow." She surveyed the dregs of the party that blanketed the living room and closed her eyes. "I think I'll just sleep through all the cleaning."

Slipping out of her purple satin heels, she added, "Can I get anyone anything?" The invitation was unanimously refused. "So, Amanda," Kitty lifted her long fall of blond hair, "Luke has been telling me that he finally has furniture. I envy your decorating skills. I wouldn't know where to start."

Amanda frowned. "Your place is lovely. I—"

She was interrupted by the other woman's laughter. "I bought the model. The condo came completely furnished. It made everything so much easier." Kitty snuggled against Lucas' side, her small chin resting on his shoulder. "I could never understand why Luke wanted to waste his money on that dilapidated old house when there were plenty of modern, new condos right in town and—"

"Lucas bought a lovely piece of property, Kitty," Wade's deep voice interjected. "I've seen your land." He turned toward Lucas. "It's quite valuable."

Lucas gave a negligent shrug. "Value wasn't my prime concern. I liked the area, the pond, the tranquillity. The basic lay of the house was attractive."

"Now, it's stunning," Amanda supplied. "Lucas had been sending me photos of all the remodeling, but seeing it in the flesh, so to speak, really took my breath away."

Kitty's lips formed a childish pout. "Well, maybe I just better see for myself what this big love affair with your place is all about, Luke."

"Not tonight." He gave her a tired smile, his eyes narrowing on his watch. "I'm beat. It's been a long two days. Shall we head home, Amanda?"

Wade stood up, insinuating his broad-shouldered physique in front of Lucas'. Extending his hand to Amanda, his fingers threaded between hers as she rose. "I'll be calling you."

Her silver eyes radiated with pleasure. "Please do."

Amanda's tired anatomy melted into the comfortable confines of the Fiat's brown leather bucket seat. "I think all the painting is finally catching up to me." She shook off her third yawn. "I'm sorry I didn't get your room finished."

"No one asked you to kill yourself."

She grimaced in the dark, attributing his brusque tone to fatigue. "Kitty is darling. Very friendly, very outgoing, very affectionate. I like her."

Lucas merely grunted. His fingers began punching the buttons on the radio. Not finding anything that appealed, he switched it off. He coughed and cleared his throat. "It seems you made the same impression on Wade Lloyd." Hands that gripped the steering wheel were damp with sweat despite the car's comfortable climate.

She twisted in the seat. "I hope so. Wade's very attractive. I liked him."

"You seem to have a distinct talent for seduction," came his curt retort.

"Really? And here I was afraid I had lost the knack." Her voice was a sinuous purr.

"Well, you haven't. If anything, it's been perfected with *age*." He overemphasized the last word.

Amanda arched a well-shaped brow. "Well, Lucas," her hand curved against his upper arm, giving a little warning squeeze, "you know, a woman doesn't really reach her prime until she's in her thirties. I've only just begun!"

"Thank you, Masters and Johnson." He ignored her laughter at his childish outburst. "I'm sure Wade Lloyd would be only too happy to prime your pump."

"I just may let him."

"What happened to the prim Victorian attitude you're always so proud of?" he said, sneering.

Amanda's mouth twisted in a wry grin. Lucas was certainly taking her to task just because she found a new man interesting. "I didn't attack Wade, did I? For all I know he may not even call. Maybe that's just his line."

"You know damn well he'll call. You have that effect."

"Effect! Me? Lucas, you know I'm always the same. I

don't become a different person when I'm with a man. Either they like Amanda Wyatt or they don't."

"There's no doubt that Wade liked you, Amanda." Lucas reached over and snapped the radio back to life. Willie Nelson managed to fill in the silence.

Amanda inhaled a luxurious breath of morning air, bare feet wriggling in the dew-washed grass. She reached into the plastic laundry basket and shook out another shirt. The rope strung between two trees was rapidly filling with damp clothes.

Gray eyes roamed the length of the line where towels and sheets billowed like miniature sails and where masculine and feminine articles rippled in the gusty breeze. Shirts were clipped to blouses, slacks hung next to jeans, but Lucas' collection of colorful bikini briefs rivaled Amanda's more moderate pastel panties.

Two yellow plastic clothespins opened their jaws to grip red briefs trimmed in navy. Amanda remembered something her mother had once said. "The way to tell if you're really in love with a man is to ask yourself if you could wash his underwear." Shaking her head, she dismissed the silly thought and reached in the basket for her nightgown.

"You're up early this morning." Lucas' sleep-graveled voice interrupted Amanda's cheery humming.

Peering between two chocolate bath towels, she smiled at him. "I saw the sun shining and decided to tackle the laundry." His brown hair was touseled, cheeks and jaw darkened by an overnight growth of beard. Well-worn jeans and a sleeveless gray sweat shirt clothed his tall athletic frame. "I made French toast. It's warming in the oven."

He grunted and cleared his throat. "Why the fuss? Coffee and toast are just fine."

"I wanted to give your day a happy start." One gray eye winked. "I knew you went to bed on the wrong side; I just wanted to make sure you didn't wake up in the same humor."

At Lucas' unintelligible reply, Amanda laughed, linked her arm through his and guided him back into the house. "I don't know why I even bother to talk to you. You're not fit for man nor beast until ten." She tapped the stove clock before picking up the percolator. "You still have thirty minutes to go."

Through half-closed hazel eyes, Lucas watched her organize his breakfast. Coffee filled his oversized pottery mug, one scoop of sugar and a dollop of milk were added; a plate of French toast dripping with maple syrup was placed on the eating bar along with utensils and a napkin.

He had always envied Amanda's ability to function at full volume early in the morning. Laundry done, an excellent breakfast prepared and she was dressed to paint. Today's T-shirt read: *Parts of me are nearly perfect.* Lucas had to smile; that slogan was so appropriate.

Her ancient cut-offs emphasized rounded buttocks and long, slender legs; the short-sleeved cotton shirt was tied under full breasts to reveal a flat midriff and the delicate muscles that rippled along graceful, bare arms.

"Lucas—" Amanda's voice jarred his musings, his fork skidded against the syrup-slick plate, sending two squares of golden toast bread slopping onto the counter.

"Sorry," she said and grimaced, turning her attention back to loading the dishwasher.

Her busy figure drew him like a magnet. His dark gaze flowed along her erogenous terrain, devouring each curve and soft swell. Hazel eyes traced the sinuous sweep of spine, the arched *derrière* and the firm thighs.

The pulse in his throat began to pound and grow, his breathing came rapid and shallow. The erotic atmosphere created by his mind began building tension again. Lucas found fascination with the enigma that was Amanda.

Her charm had captivated and enthralled. The attraction of her kept building; but his feelings were more than platonic. He desired her as a man desires a woman.

While Lucas knew Amanda's mind, he had little knowledge of her body. Suddenly that was what he craved most. He wanted more than holiday kisses, casual hand-holding and brother-sister tussles. He was anxious to taste and explore the very essence of her femininity, share the joys of physical love.

But were his feelings the result of years of their look-but-don't-touch relationship? Or did he really want to set their friendship on fire?

Confusion and shame melded into guilt, and Lucas swallowed his thoughts as quickly as he gulped his coffee. What he needed was physical labor—some good, old-fashioned exercise to sweat out his troublesome emotions.

Amanda moved to take his empty plate. "What's on your schedule for today?"

He stood up. "I thought I'd go out and mow the back forty." Lucas was surprised how normal his voice sounded.

She laughed and shook her head. "With that riding tractor, it's almost an insult to call mowing the lawn work."

"Hey, we can switch," came his amiable offer. "I'll stay inside and paint, you can sit and ride while the sun broils your skin and melts your bones."

Pretending to ponder his suggestion, Amanda's eyes grew wide and serious. "I don't think so, Lucas. I'll stay indoors and acquire a latex glow."

They met again, four hours later. Two tired, sweat-drenched bodies stumbled into the kitchen in search of a cool drink.

Lucas twisted off a cap and handed Amanda a cold beer. "Here. This is the only thing that will take the taste of paint out of your mouth."

She readily accepted, greedily letting the cold, somewhat bitter malt liquor quench her thirst. "I'm done. Your room is a masterpiece." Amanda rubbed the perspiration-drenched bottle against her throat and around the back of her neck. I put a coat of Minwax on the baseboards; that natural woodgrain trim was too beautiful to cover."

He leaned against the refrigerator, tossing his twist-off cap toward the sink. "Well, the yard is mowed and trimmed, the stalls have been cleaned and the car and truck washed."

Amanda watched his Adam's apple bob up and down as he drank. "Does this mean we're both finished for the day?" At Lucas' affirmative nod, she exhaled in relief. "My energy is in great need of revitalization."

"Hmm." His dark eyes appraised the paint-spattered copper curls that were crowned with a red bandanna rolled into a sweatband. "Do you have enough energy to pack something for lunch while I saddle the horses? We can head down to the pond and cool off with a swim."

"I did make some fried chicken this morning and a potato salad. It was supposed to be dinner, but . . ." Amanda rubbed her hands together. "Why don't we have dinner now and eat lunch tonight. As far as a swimsuit goes"—she examined spangled legs and arms—"I'd have to shower and change." Her lips compressed together. "Lucas, I'm jumping in as is!"

Food and drink were packed in two ice-filled canvas carry-alls and slung across the saddles. After being confined in the barn during the inclement weather, the horses were eager for an adventurous outing. Buttercup and Maizey snorted and pranced in delighted appreciation across the rolling pasture to the pond.

"Come on in, the water's perfect!" Lucas' voice called. He waved, then proceeded to dive like a seal into the clear depths.

Amanda brushed another tuft of fuzzy cotton seeds off the picnic blanket, carefully anchoring the material with four good-size rocks. "A woman's work is never done," she muttered, righting his boots and neatly folding the sweat shirt Lucas had discarded before he had swung his jeans-clad body Tarzan-style into the pond.

"Mandy, aren't you coming in?"

"Ready or not . . ." Amanda double-checked her pockets for anything dissolvable. Not to be outdone by Lucas' athletic prowess, she too decided to make a dramatic entrance into the water. "Here I come!"

Gripping the thick sisal rope that looped over a strong

cottonwood branch, Amanda ran back, lifted her feet off the ground and was propelled up and over the middle of the pond. A few seconds of giddy vertigo were instantly corrected by a sober dunking into the frigid water.

"Lucas!" She screamed his name, shaking the water from her face and hair.

"What?" His innocent face was blinked into focus.

"You wretched creature!" Amanda's hands settled against his broad shoulders, her narrowed gray eyes slanted a warning message. "This pond must be fed by a polar ice cap!" Her teeth gave an exaggerated chatter.

Broad shoulders gave a lazy shrug. "Seems fine to me." Her Cheshire-cat grin was the last thing Lucas saw before he was deftly submerged.

The crisp, crystal lake proved to be the perfect panacea to their work-exhausted bodies and psyches. They frolicked like children in the invigorating water, trying to catch the sunfish and perch that quickly darted around them, or swimming alongside one of the large rock turtles that kept disappearing into its hard-shelled home.

A game of dares ensued. Lucas and Amanda turned into acrobats, making the rope into their trapeze. While graceful in mind, their somersaults and swan dives proved more often to be belly flops and ungainly stunts.

Physically tired but spiritually rejuvenated, they dragged themselves onto the grassy banks to embrace the healing strength supplied by the sunlight that filtered through the verdant broadleaf canopy of cottonwood trees.

"I don't think Ringling Brothers is going to beat a path to your door," Amanda announced, lazily stretching her arms over her head and closing her eyes. "You lowered the water level in the pond by two feet!"

"You should talk! I always thought you were poetry in motion, but Mandy . . ." His tongue clicked an accusing message against the roof of his mouth.

Her warm, full-bodied laugh serenaded his ears. Lucas turned his head, opening one sleepy hazel eye to survey Amanda's supine form. Suddenly he was completely alert, all fatigue forgotten. Moments ago they had played like innocent children in their Garden of Eden, but now some invading serpent touched the animal in him.

Her delicate eyelids were closed, her face tilted up toward the sky. Lucas studied the tender curve of an ear, glimpsed through teasing water-darkened tendrils. His dark gaze watched the steady rise and fall of her full breasts beneath the clinging soaked T-shirt; urgent nipples pointedly proclaimed a need for warmth beneath a bra that had been rendered useless by her swim.

"This was a brilliant idea, Lucas." Amanda yawned and forced her eyes open. "I bet you're as hungry as I am."

"More so," Lucas agreed, letting one last visual examination feed and assuage his sensual appetite.

Golden brown fried chicken, potato salad, carrots, celery and tomatoes were distributed on paper plates and heartily consumed. They sat Indian style on the green Army blanket, concentrating on refueling their energy with food; the companionable silence was broken by an occasional whinny from the tethered horses or a mockingbird feasting on cotton fruit and seeds.

Amanda exhaled a contented sigh, her eyes monopolized by the beauty of her surroundings. "Starting tomorrow we get an extra hour of sunlight to enjoy all this." She gave Lucas a grateful smile. "Coming here was just what I needed."

"I'm glad, Mandy." He leaned over to tap her nose with his carrot stick. "It's been a long time since we were together; I'm really getting used to having you around."

Mouth open, her even white teeth snapped apart the bright orange vegetable. "I will admit I haven't given the shop or myself much thought." Amanda's expression turned serious. "I've been very happy here with you, Lucas." She grinned suddenly. "I may turn into 'the woman who came to dinner' and just stay and stay and stay . . ." Her voice trailed off in amusement.

"I wouldn't mind that at all." He strived to make his tone light but failed, at least to his own ears.

She tossed him two red Delicious apples. "I brought these for our trusty steeds."

While Lucas ambled off to give Buttercup and Maizey an afternoon snack, Amanda began to pick up the littered remains of their picnic. Her labors were resoundly interrupted by a manly cry. "Lucas!" She scrambled to her feet, running to his limping figure. "What happened?"

"A wasp." He was hopping, foot in hand, trying to examine his toe. "I think the stinger is still in there."

Amanda looked at his pain-contorted features, feeling an empathetic stabbing in her own foot. "You aren't allergic to them, are you?" At his negative shake, she took a calming breath. "Okay, sit down. Let me see."

"It hurts," Lucas announced, his deep voice sounding slightly higher than it usually did.

"I'll be careful," she placated her patient. Amanda filled a paper cup from the pond, letting the cool water wash away the dirt from his well-padded big toe. "You're right," she said, looking up from an intense examination of his size ten appendage, "the stinger is still in there. I'll have to pull it out."

A low moan escaped him. "Do you know what you're doing? I don't want to end up with gangrene and—"

"Men! What babies!" Amanda flexed her thumb and index finger, eyeing the considerable length of nail that would play tweezers. "Now hold still," she cautioned, and with a single quick, clean movement, she eliminated the tiny black sliver of venom. "All done." Again she cleansed the reddened digit, then began to mix the rest of the water with dirt.

"What are you doing now?" Lucas came up on his elbows to watch her actions.

"I'm making a mudpack." She proceeded to bury not only his toe but also his entire left foot beneath a castle of cool, moist earth. "It's an age-old poultice to reduce swelling and ease pain." Her hands happily patted the giant structure. Amanda smiled encouragingly. "Doesn't that feel better?"

"No."

She laughed, rinsed her hands in the pond and played with his right foot. "Don't worry, Lucas," her voice was low and teasing, "you have nine others." Dark lashes sheltered glittering eyes. "This little piggy went to market, this little piggy stayed home," she played the childish game with his toes, "and this little piggy went weeeee," her finger ran down his sole, curved up his jean covered leg, over shin, knee, thigh and hipbone to come to a final halt in the indentation of his hair-shrouded navel, "all the way home."

He grabbed Amanda's wrist, easily hauling her laughing form the full length of his body. Two large hands settled her comfortably against his chest. "Nurses are not supposed to torture their patients," Lucas admonished. But he found himself luxuriating in the punishment her soft curves inflicted against his masculine frame.

Amanda's elbows settled in the sand on either side of his head. Her fingertips traced his thick, dark moustache, then playfully pulled down his full lower lip. "Poor Luke." Her hands splayed against his warm, sun-golden flesh, palms rubbing amid the black fur that blanketed his muscular chest.

"Please," he gave her buttocks a warning squeeze, "you know how I hate that nickname!"

"Why don't you tell Kitty?"

"I have," his mouth twisted. "She thinks it's—"

"Cute," Amanda supplied, eyes wide and innocent.

A low growl emanated. "Listen, Amanda Juliet—"

Feminine lashes fluttered coquettishly. "Yes, Lucas Anthony?" Amanda's knuckle teased the niche in his cheek until it formed the dimple he had always hated. "How's the foot doing?"

He smiled into her smoky eyes, enjoying the last few moments of this intimate sojourn. "Better than new. I bet I can even get my boot on."

They took the long way home, enjoying the western horizon that was stained with a mystic mauve glow. "How about setting your alarm for a predawn ride," Lucas invited as they reigned the horses for a final look at the valley. "You should see all this early in the morning, Mandy;

everything is still fogged with sleep until the sun flares in the sky. The spectacular display lasts an hour."

"We can pack up a breakfast," she decided, giving Maizey's neck a soothing rub. "Thermos of coffee and some muffins."

"Sounds perfect," he said and smiled before cueing Buttercup toward home.

Lucas came in through the patio doorway just as Amanda had finished loading the dishwasher. "Don't turn that on," he warned. "I'm headed for the shower."

"Hey," her hands settled on her hips. "What about ladies first? I still have to chip all this paint off of me."

They were still arguing when the telephone beeped an intermission. "Hello," Lucas listened for a moment, then a muscle moved ominously in his cheek. "It's for you." He handed the beige receiver to Amanda. "Wade Lloyd."

"Hello, Wade." Her well-modulated voice drifted a harmonious greeting across the line. "It's lovely to hear from you."

"This is my sixth call to you today," Wade announced. "I was just about to give up."

"I'm glad you didn't." She motioned for Lucas to head for the shower, but he stubbornly didn't budge. Amanda turned her back, the cord wrapped around her waist.

"I was hoping you'd say that." His tone relayed his pleasure. "I had a business meeting scheduled for tonight, and when it fell through I found my thoughts focused on you. I'm hoping you'll say yes to joining me for dinner tonight."

"I'd love to. What time will you pick me up?"

"About ninety minutes? I . . . I apologize for the short notice, Amanda. I—"

"Don't give it a second thought, Wade," she soothed his concern. "I just adore spur-of-the-moment plans. Where are you taking me?"

"You were hardly spur-of-the-moment, Amanda." His deep voice held a note of intimacy. "As a matter of fact, you've been on my mind all night long. But we can discuss that over a Chinese dinner."

"Marvelous." The word fairly purred into the phone.

"See you shortly." Amanda untwisted herself from the cord and smiled at Lucas. "I'm afraid you're on your own tonight, boy." Her tongue clicked against her teeth. "I've got a date!"

Chapter Seven

"MAY I COMPLIMENT your attire." Wade's vibrant voice was close to Amanda's ear as his large hand filled the small of her back, making his masculine presence known as the sartorially perfect waiter led them to a corner booth.

"When one is taken to the Jade Garden, one dresses appropriately," she bantered with ease, fingers flowing along the mandarin neckline of her blouse.

His blue eyes grew even brighter, sculpting the lush curves that moved beneath her sizzly Charmeuse silk top and matching slinky satin pants. "I find myself thinking of all the interesting places I can take you, so I can be continually dazzled by your sense of style."

"I'm afraid I packed a very limited wardrobe."

"I have a hunch your creative imagination is endless."

The evening, Amanda decided as she slid into the red leather cushioned booth, was starting out a perfect ten, and there was every indication it might reach even higher. The atmosphere in the Jade Garden was quiet, cozy and romantic. Soft music, candles flickering beneath dainty silkscreen lanterns and the privacy curtain that surrounded their banquette made for a perfect tête-à-tête.

There had been, however, a small crack in the fortune cookie. Amanda gave an inward grimace, her eyes studying the detailed menu. Lucas. The man acted like a two-year-old being left with a baby-sitter for the first time. He hadn't even been civil enough to greet Wade at the door.

Strange, her father had always acted the same way when she had gone out on dates. Her mother said he was jealous—thinking perhaps this male would replace him in her life. She exhaled a confused sigh. She wondered if this were typical "big brother" jealousy. Men! Weren't they the ones who said women were complex and complicated?

Four masculine fingers pulled down the glossy black-covered menu. "Let me guess." Wade's knowledgeable smile strove to remove the creases that etched her previously smooth forehead. "You're having trouble deciding which one to order from Column A, Column B and Column C."

Silver lids lowered to shade-matching irises. "I'm going to put myself totally in your capable hands." Her husky voice issued the invitation. Amanda shifted her legs. Their knees touched, but neither of them broke physical contact.

The waiter's beaming moon-face appeared between the curtains. Without hesitation, Wade ordered seven suns and a moon for two, wonton soup, rice, tea and fortune cookies. "You won't be disappointed," he promised Amanda after the waiter had bowed his leave. "The food here is authentic and excellent."

Reaching for the ice water, Amanda took a moment to reassess her initial reaction to the new man who had entered her perimeter. She found that the second appraisal reaffirmed her first impression. Wade was attractive but not overtly handsome, casual and relaxed yet self-assured and polished. Amanda liked his smile, his voice, his stature, but most of all she liked his eyes.

"Now tell me about your meeting that was canceled." Her lips issued a subtle smile. "I'd like to send them a thank-you note."

His appreciative laugh enhanced the spirit of fun. "You are wonderful for a man's ego, Amanda." Wade's hand covered hers, long, blunt fingers entwined with feminine, polished ones. "But I insist that you tell me about your day."

"I finished painting Lucas' bedroom while he worked around the property, then we took to the pond on horseback for a swim and a picnic." Silk-shrouded shoulders gave a casual shrug. "Not all that interesting," came her coy rejoinder. Amanda found she was thriving on his rapt attention and tried to prolong her enjoyment.

"Interesting and intriguing." His thumb made little circles against the sensitive skin on her wrist. Wade found growing resentment toward the table that made body contact so restrictive. "You already know I'm allergic to tomatoes," he coaxed lightly. "I want the same ammunition."

Her smile sought to captivate. "I'm afraid I have no known allergies, Mr. Lloyd." Amanda grinned, her tone less little-girlish. "Which is very lucky, since I adore creole and Cajun cooking and all other types, for that matter."

"Where do you live? What's it like?"

Her answer was stayed while white lotus bowls of steaming, fragrant soup were placed before them. "I have a very nice townhouse on Lake Pontchartrain. I bought it four years ago when the area was first being developed." Her spoon stirred the golden liquid, toying with the small meat-filled dumplings.

"All the units are basically the same, but inside I created a world of my own." Amanda cleared her throat. "I hadn't realized how much I missed my home." Her self-conscious laugh gave way to a crimson blush.

Wade's eyes grew soft. "I wish I could embrace those same feelings toward my own place." At her look of inquiry, he continued. "I bought two condo units in Prestonwood, the same area Kitty lives in. I rent one out and use the other. But I, too, had some unknown decorator furnish the place, and it really just serves a function."

He added crispy fried noodles to his soup. "Perhaps after you're through with Lucas' house you can work your magic touch in mine?"

"I'm flattered." Amanda poured greenish-brown oolong tea into scenic pattern china cups. "Maybe you should inspect the results first," she advised with a smile.

"If Lucas wouldn't mind the intrusion?"

Her red linen napkin came up to mask her frown. "I'll see about talking him into a housewarming party," she said as she moved her empty bowl to one side. "Although it may have to wait until I find a dining-room set."

"I was really very surprised when Lucas and Kitty got together."

"I don't understand." Gray eyes blinked questioningly. "They looked the perfect couple last night."

"I've known Kitty for three years," Wade replied, broad shoulders relaxing into the leather seat. "She's a very young twenty-four . . . very immature, although not in her work habits," he added hastily. "I mean in attitude. Kitty is still caught up in images, out to prove she's free, anxious to have it all, have it right now, this instant. And Lucas is . . . well . . ." His hand massaged his jaw. "I have the feeling Lucas and I are very much alike. We appreciate less *nouveau* and are captivated by the real thing."

His sapphire gaze focused on Amanda. Her halo of brown curls reflected burnished lights; soft tendrils coiled around ears that invited sensual whispers. Wade found a vulnerability that was quite alluring in her features. The tender curve of her cheek, the soft, full lips, and those marvelous smoky irises. He wanted to see them darken with passion—for him. How in the world could Crosse have gotten so lucky? He envied the man. Envied? Hell, he was jealous!

A rueful smile twisted Wade's firm, masculine lips. "Here I am going on about two people who aren't at all my concern, when I really have yet to learn all I can about you."

"Let me see, where shall I begin?" Amanda gave an exaggerated sigh, her fingertip bouncing in contemplation against her chin. "I was born on a dark and stormy night," her husky voice intoned, eyes sparking with mischievous flames.

Their shared amusement was interrupted by the entrée. Wade politely dismissed the waiter and served the food himself. As the silver chafing dish cover was lifted, a delicious aroma filled the air, instantly arousing their taste buds; the colorful main dish was no less pleasing to the eye.

"You certainly did not exaggerate the cuisine." Amanda offered her plate and was rewarded with crisp vegetables cooked in a wok, boned chicken, jumbo broiled shrimps, lobster chunks and delicate strips of pork over a base of fluffy white rice.

A mutual silence enveloped the couple while they sampled the elegant Chinese fare. Filled tea cups clicked together in a respectful toast to the chef.

"You just can't leave me lost in a storm," Wade remarked, enhancing the snow peas with soy sauce. "Finish your story."

Amanda smiled. "You certainly are a determined man." She speared a slice of pork. "I am an only child and an Army brat." She let that sink in while she chewed. "My family moved around the various bases in this country and we spent eighteen months in Germany. My parents are retired now and live in North Carolina."

"What were you like as a child? How did you get interested in fashion design?" Wade pressed, anxious to sample her life.

"As a child, well"—her fork sifted through the rice, looking for another lobster tidbit—"I was tall, sassy, stubborn, independent. Much the same as I am today." Amanda found she was holding back little intimacies that she usually laughed at. Strange, she hadn't with Lucas, and twelve years ago she had been at an age when such youthful frailties were so all-important.

Sweetened, pungent tea cleansed her palate and gave her time to arrange her thoughts. "I guess I started out being interested in fashion the way a lot of girls do." At his arched dark brow, Amanda supplied: "Designing doll clothes. I started with crayons on paper towels, graduated to scraps of material and a needle and thread, then continued with patterns and a sewing machine.

"I was very artistic, had a good eye for color and shapes and—" Her hand made a graceful gesture. "I spent two years studying art at NYU, two years at the Fashion Institute of Technology, then won a scholarship to Couture School in Paris, which was where I learned I knew absolutely nothing." Amanda expelled a low chuckle. "I returned to New York, became an assistant chief designer on

Seventh Avenue. Did six collections in three seasons and was scared to death after each one.

"Indigestion, insomnia and headaches became a way of life, and when I didn't have one of the above, I got one wondering why I didn't have it in the first place." Her tongue moistened dry lips. "But for all that insanity, I reaped great personal rewards and many, many friends. I think it was the most exciting time in my life, save when I first started my own business."

Wade had long abandoned his dinner, savoring instead the myriad of emotions that regaled Amanda's softly flushed features. "Tell me about that too." His tone had an urgency that surprised them both.

She hesitated for a moment, trying to decide if he was being polite or sincere. Amanda banked on the last. "The transition from designer to businesswoman was quite accidental. I was in my bank waiting for traveler's checks when I overheard a lawyer talking to one of the bank officers. The lawyer had an estate to sell that included a dress shop in the French Quarter. I sassily"—she gave him an impertinent wink—"interrupted. We adjourned our discussion to lunch. Instead of going to Paradise Island as I had planned, I went to New Orleans and fell in love with the shop on Royal Street.

"I called Lucas for legal advice and he flew over. We spent days going over figures with the bank and finally I signed my name on innumerable dotted lines." Amanda's gray eyes were shrouded in memories. "My insomnia, headaches and indigestion came back and I was," her laughter dispelled her serious tone, "higher than a kite."

The scattered remains of their dinner were deftly removed. A fresh pot of tea, orange sherbet and two fortune cookies commanded attention.

"I get the feeling that the word *was* figures prominently in your life right now," Wade ventured, quickly becoming susceptible to the inflections in her voice. "Isn't the shop doing well? I know the economy puts a lot of stress on the small-businessman."

The orange sherbet felt cool and tart against her throat.

"Rags 'n' Riches is doing exceptionally well." Amanda was finding it difficult not to brag and added, "Our gross sales have been running three times the national average. About six hundred dollars per square foot of selling space." She paused to sip her tea before continuing.

"This year's payroll alone equals the gross sales volume the store did ten years ago. I'm importing more fashions from Europe due to the demands of my customers, and I've added jewelry, scarves, leather goods and other accessories plus my own talent when someone requests a one-of-a-kind design."

His fruit ice disintegrated the instant it touched his tongue. "That's . . . that's quite an achievement." Wade didn't have to feign surprise. He had never expected Amanda Wyatt to be such a competent businesswoman. "I always thought women would buy and wear just about anything."

Her tone was as acerbic as their dessert. "Wade, that's a very old-fashioned, chauvinistic statement."

He opened his mouth, then quickly closed it. His silver-laced head shook with self-inflicted mortification. "I apologize." His finger inched away the tan shirt collar that had become quite constricted. "I confess I'm amazed at your prowess. When we talked about the boutique last night, I sloughed off your remarks to pride."

"I'm afraid I'm addicted to pride on occasion." Amanda relaxed her defensive attitude, tempering her further comments with undeniable charm. "I think of the store in a very maternal way."

"Like the lioness protecting her cub," he offered.

Amanda abandoned her spoon to her half-empty dish. "An overly protective lioness," came her rueful admission. "Even though I have some very talented, capable people working for me, and this is always the slack season . . ." She shook her head. "It was like pulling the proverbial tooth for me to leave."

Wade's perceptive blue gaze searched Amanda's face, seeking the vitality that previously radiated. "You were afraid to find just how well the cub could manage without his mother."

"Yes. I've been avoiding the truth for a long time." Her hand ruffled the copper waves that sculpted her head. "I settled into a comfortable routine, got used to not having the fears that plagued my psyche and tried to ignore the boredom."

"We're a lot alike," his voice was low and compelling, "thriving on a challenge, growing under excitement, slightly reckless, harboring a bit of a gambler's instinct."

"Not too reckless," Amanda countered calmly. "I like to hedge my bets." She picked up the lotus bowl that housed two golden cookies. "Your fortune."

He hesitated a moment, then made his choice. Wade broke the crisp, edible container and extracted a small printed message. His lips twisted into a soft smile. "You will meet a tall, dark-haired stranger who will change your life."

"You're kidding! Let me see." Laughing at his verse, she reached for her own. Amanda's expression turned serious. "Much more the Confucius saying: Own your soul but share your heart."

"I hope you believe in these ancient messages. So far mine has come true." Wade lifted his teacup, toasting her presence. "How are your feet?"

"Both are alive and well."

"There's a very nice lounge around the corner. Think you'd enjoy some music and dancing?"

Amanda's diamond-bright eyes glowed in acceptance. "That sounds wonderful."

After-dinner cognacs were served in balloon snifters warmed by candle flames; the heated, aromatic French brandy echoed the sensuous nuances of the Hideout. The lounge seemed wrapped in voluptuous intimacy.

Private booths were shielded by stained-glass dividers; electric candles flickered in antique sconces on rich stucco walls, casting a twilight glow over the patrons. Hushed conversations, enhanced by exotic libations, were sparked with sporadic laughter. The only outside invaders were the soft sounds of piano, drums, bass and guitar—earthy, erotic music that solicited more physical contact.

With every passing moment, Wade became more absorbed with the scarlet fantasy that was Amanda Wyatt. She was an original; she created instead of mimicked. At times she seemed cool and serene, then she was suddenly flamboyant and frankly feminine. He found the dichotomy decidedly stimulating.

Atmosphere and music created a sensuous spell that could no longer be ignored. Wade drew Amanda into his arms; their bodies easily duplicated the throbbing rhythm. "We make perfect partners," he whispered. The haunting scent of her floral perfume seemed to Wade to harmonize with the romantic ballad. His hand moved up her arm, over her slender back, then traveled the sensuous neck-to-waist curve of her spine. Wade couldn't tell the difference between silken blouse and satin skin.

Amanda's fingers smoothed the lapels on his brown glen plaid suit jacket, pressing lightly into the luxurious material of his shirt. The heat radiating from his flesh fanned the slumbering embers in her blood.

She snuggled closer, supple curves sculpted against his rugged proportions, anxious to feel the wonders of his hard, athletic body. "You're an excellent dancer." Her husky voice excited his inner ear; her own sense of smell was penetrated by the odor of crisp, classic cologne.

Wade pulled back slightly. "This was the quickest way I could think to get you this close."

Ebony pupils looked circled in diamonds. "I like a man of action, a man who knows what he wants."

His right hand abandoned her waist to trace the graceful sweep of her neck; one blunt finger lifted her chin. With mutual unspoken consent, his head lowered the scant few inches needed to bridge the ensuing gap of silence.

Oblivious to the other couples who populated the dance floor, their lips and tongues played a gentle, probing game. The pressure of Wade's mouth and hands created delicious currents that tortured Amanda's sane resolve. An inward flow of sensations, twisting from stomach to thigh, slowly but inexorably began to build.

Amanda ultimately broke their intimate connection. "I . . . I think we're providing the floor show." Her voice was as unsteady as her pulse.

"I'm sorry." Wade rested his forehead against hers, his palms closing tightly against her shoulder blades, pressing her close to his chest. "This is crazy." His lips twisted in a rueful smile. "You've made me feel like a young boy. I want to show off just for you."

"Wade," her gaze locked into his, "I'm not a tease. I'm not a flirt. I don't rush into relationships. I am very, very careful."

"I admire your candor and respect your values." His expression was serious. "I certainly hope you won't mind if I continue my advances?"

Amanda's lips whispered against his. "I'd be insulted if you didn't."

They danced until the band had exhausted their talent and time. Then Wade and Amanda adjourned to the solitary cocoon of their booth, talking and lingering over another brandy. The barrel-chested bartender pointedly tabled the surrounding chairs and began to mop the floors in a final, unsubtle attempt to bid the couple good night.

Amanda curled sideways in the front seat of Wade's pewter Cadillac. Her hand curved around his upper arm, reaching out in a warm expression of intimacy. She encouraged him to talk about his work and found Wade a delightful raconteur. A pleasurable invisible web was spun between them.

In the end it was Lucas who dissolved their magical evening. His newly acquired porch light flooded the yard with two hundred watts of critical, pontifical illumination.

"The last time I ran into something like this"—Wade gestured toward the daylight-bright courtyard as he helped Amanda from the car—"was when I was sixteen and dating a Baptist minister's daughter."

"And did she get a handshake instead of a kiss?" Amanda inquired. Her arm slid around his waist to match his gesture.

"She did." He stopped and turned her toward him. "But you won't." Gentle fingertips stroked Amanda's eyelids closed, enveloping her in erotic darkness.

Wade's mouth devoured her lips. His probing tongue conquered the lush interior, savoring juices more potent than the aged brandy he had consumed. His hands roamed freely over her back, their bodies reveling in the close contact.

Her breasts and pelvis burned their womanly imprint against his virile strength. Body heat began to build; small jolts quaked her nerves. Where they touched—shoulders, chest, hips, thighs—everything seemed electrified.

Their energies were somehow transmitted to a less insulated object. The porch light exploded, sending a shower of glass raining against the concrete.

Wade shook his head, his voice etched with amusement. "Lucas must have this place booby-trapped. I think that's my cue to leave."

"Good morning." Amanda yawned the greeting, sleepily navigating her lilac-kimono-robed body into the kitchen.

"Good afternoon, you mean." Lucas deliberately opened the percolator, took out the basket, emptied the grounds and liquid into the sink's garbage disposal and flipped the switch.

"It's only eleven."

"You forgot to set your clock ahead." He finished rinsing the metal pot. "You also forgot to set your alarm for our breakfast ride."

She grimaced. "I'm sorry, Lucas." Amanda attempted a smile. "We can plan it again. There's a new dawn every day."

He grunted something unintelligible, his dark gaze shifting to her flushed face and touseled hair. Lucas took a deep breath and refilled the pot with fresh water and coffee. "How was your evening?" The question was reluctantly asked.

"I had a wonderful time. I like Wade. I like him very much."

The percolator hit the electric burner with a thud. "Don't you think he moves too fast?" Lucas blurted, shoving his hands in the back pockets of his jeans. "After all, what do you know about him?"

"He's allergic to tomatoes and loves Chinese food." Amanda ignored Lucas' mumbled "communist." Her gray eyes caught the sunlight. "He's an excellent dancer and a scintillating conversationalist." She winked happily. "And he's a great kisser."

"Don't be crude."

A burst of giggles erupted from her throat. "Crude! Lucas, what about that porch light? Even my father never went that far!"

"I put in a bulb that was lying around," he grumbled, passing her a coffee mug. "It was too large and blew up."

"I know. We thought we'd done it!"

Eyes narrowed, jaw tightened. Lucas gave her a quelling stare.

Amanda sighed; her fingers drummed against the butcher block eating bar. "Why didn't you call Kitty last night?"

"I did. I got her answering machine. I got it again this morning. She usually has to work on Sundays hostessing open houses."

"Then don't take your male frustrations out on me," she warned. "I already have parents, and I don't need a guardian."

"I have no intentions of becoming your guardian."

She cleared her throat, softening her expression and her tone. "Lucas, you wanted me to have fun, to meet new people. I combined the two in the form of Wade Lloyd. You should be happy."

He opened his mouth, then closed it. What was he supposed to say? He wanted to yell that Lloyd didn't deserve her, didn't have the right to become involved. But he didn't. He couldn't. Lucas knew he didn't have that right, either!

Amanda heard him mutter something about "possession being eleven points in the law" as he stalked past her and headed outdoors. Waiting for the toast to pop up, the telltale shattering of wood penetrated through the screened windows. Lucas, Amanda decided, seemed to turn into Paul Bunyan whenever he had a problem. She wondered when this phase of brotherly jealousy would wear off.

Amanda had intended to set the coffee table for dinner but then decided Lucas wouldn't appreciate sitting "Chinese style." She did prepare one of his favorite meals—beef stroganoff over noodles, with garlic bread and hearts of lettuce salad—again letting the slate fireplace hearth function as the dining table when a late-afternoon shower made eating outdoors impossible.

"This is delicious." Lucas settled into a more comfortable position on one of the new gold upholstered floor pillows.

Her lips curved into a happy smile. He had spent the entire afternoon in total silence while hooking up the stereo system. Amanda was glad he was talking! "I took some window measurements in the bedrooms today. I was thinking about shutters? Varnishing them to match the woodwork and sewing a valance?"

His fork stirred through the rich sour cream sauce, spearing a tender beef chunk and a mushroom cap. "I like it. But I don't have a sewing machine."

"I can rent one. It'll only take a day's work. I'd like to do it."

Lucas took a deep breath, his eyes focused on the low, leaping flames. "Look, Mandy, I'm . . . I'm sorry about this morning. That was lousy of me. You didn't deserve that." He wanted to make a joke about being jealous so he could check her reaction, but his instincts warned him to hold his tongue.

Her hand slid under his jaw, deftly turning his face toward her. "Lucas, I'm used to your moods. I think I've sampled them all, just the way you've always tuned into mine." Amanda's fingertips gently massaged away the stress lines that etched his eyes and the bridge of his nose. An irreverent grin transformed her pensive features. "Besides, Lucas," her voice a low whisper, "love means never having to say you're sorry."

He made a grab for her, calloused fingers sliding around jade-silk-covered shoulders. "Amanda Wyatt, you are very fresh!"

"Just part of my charm," she murmured while fluttering her lashes suggestively. "Lucas," Amanda's hands curved around muscular forearms, "we've been together for a long time. I only want the best for you, too." She selected her words with care. "Is . . . is Kitty giving you a hard time? Is she playing games?" Amanda recalled that Wade had mentioned her immaturity. "She's young, maybe likes to tease." She watched Lucas' face. "Being a woman, I'll admit to playing a few tricks in my time. Maybe I can ease your mind?"

A weary hand came up to rub his face. "I'm not sure who's playing," Lucas readily confessed. "Lately we've both been picking at each other. We meet for lunch and end up with nothing to say." He turned away. "Time will tell."

Lucas had known for weeks this relationship with Kitty Byrnes was rapidly coming to an end. What was that old line: too hot not to cool down. Kitty just wasn't right—yes, the sex had been good, but he wanted more than just that. He slanted a look at Amanda, instantly knowing the *more* that he wanted.

They ate in companionable silence. Amanda tried to think of ways to lift Lucas' spirits. Funny, wasn't he the one who had done that for her? Or had it been Wade?

Her thoughts drifted back to last night. Wade had said he felt young and carefree—so had she. Laughing, flirting, sometimes serious, then rapidly nonsensical. She hadn't danced that much in years, nor had she received that much attention.

Brian Neuman never enjoyed restaurants, tripping the light fantastic, counting the stars and making silly wishes. Brian had been boring. Maybe he had infected her with that disease, too.

Even white teeth broke the crunchy crust on the heel of the garlic bread. Amanda's smoky gaze covertly surveyed the other man in her life. She had teasingly said that old love story line, but it was true—she did love Lucas. But there were many types of love, and their relationship had always been platonic.

She ruefully admitted her attitude had not been very sisterly toward Lucas. She no longer relegated him to "brother" status. Of late, he had become a fantasy lover, so real that in the magic of midnight, his remembered scent, texture, voice and touch gave him more than phantom qualifications. The thought of Lucas could make her body feel wondrous things.

Damn! For a girl who had one date in high school, a handful in college, another half dozen when she was working and one almost serious relationship, Amanda was surprised by her sudden wealth. Maybe she should treat Lucas and Wade as equals—recognize that both were attractive, accessible men.

She did the dishes by hand that night, studying the luminescent soapsuds for inspiration—it seemed to work for the women in the TV commercials! At the end of an hour, Amanda decided to follow the fortune cookie's advice: She already owned her soul, perhaps now was the time to share her heart—or, at least, let her head stop ruling it!

After tidying up the kitchen, Amanda returned to the newly furnished alcove. Lucas was comfortably ensconced in his recliner, the table lamp's low light directed on the current issue of *Law Review*.

"While the weather outside is frightful, we can still enjoy a camper's favorite dessert." She jiggled a bag of marshmallows and held up two shish kebab skewers. Her curly head nodded toward the crackling logs, eyebrows arched suggestively: "Want to play flaming gourmet?"

Lucas took a moment to add two of Amanda's favorite albums to the turntable—Lou Rawls and Barry Manilow—before joining her at the hearth. "I love having a fire at night." The brass poker revived the tapering flames. "The rains cool things off enough so I can still indulge."

"I remember lighting my fireplace in August and having the air conditioning on at the same time." She grinned engagingly. "I felt frightfully wicked and disgracefully guilty about energy conservation."

"But that didn't stop you."

"You know me too well." Amanda wiggled two plump marshmallows on each skewer. "Do you remember the last time we did this?"

His dark brows drew together for a thoughtful moment, then Lucas smiled. "My folks' place in Maine."

She nodded. "Your sister Kathy filled her cheeks like a chipmunk, and you hit them!" Her tongue clicked against the roof of her mouth. "Naughty boy!"

"Hey, weren't you the girl who trapped all those fireflies in the peanut butter jar?"

"Trying to conserve energy," came her defensive comment. "I got enough light to read by." Amanda gave him a soft smile. "Did I ever thank you enough for forcing me to go with you for those two weeks?"

"No, I don't think you did."

"Well, then," she lifted the lit confections from the fire, "allow me to re-create the moment." The gold-based blue flame that toasted the marshmallow's exterior was reflected in her clear eyes. Pursing full lips, her cool breath extinguished the glow. She pulled the spun sugar free and offered the crisp yet squishy dessert to Lucas.

His teeth scraped her fingertips in anxious consumption of the spongy morsel. His lips held her finger in place so his tongue could savor any residue. "Delicious." His husky tone conveyed a deeper meaning.

Dappled gray eyes locked into hazel ones. Amanda's mouth moistened the same finger Lucas had relinquished, then slowly proceeded to clean the dark hairs of his moustache. "Messy," she whispered, closely inspecting the results.

Of their own volition, Lucas' hands spanned her waist, masculine fingers sliding half under the silken blouse to

caress velvety skin that disappeared into the elastic band
of her black cotton slacks.

Amanda didn't pull back. Her torso leaned forward to
rest against his chest, full breasts pressed into the thin
white cotton knit shirt that covered his warm flesh. She
found herself responding to his male presence, the closeness, the excitement—they aroused her body and desires.

Play turned to passion. Her hands locked around Lucas'
head, her face tilted in silent encouragement, her mouth
parted invitingly. In a single breathtaking moment, their
lips made a tender merger. His hard tongue made a tenta-
tive inquiry and found welcome in the honeyed recesses beyond.

Fear and confusion made Lucas break contact, but his
arms still held her trembling body prisoner. "I . . . I'm not
sure how that happened."

"I wanted it," came her hushed confession, her eyes concentrating on the buttons of his shirt.

"To compare against Wade?"

"No. Am I being compared to Kitty?"

"She's been compared to you." Lucas hesitated, cleared
his throat and added, "Quite a few woman have been compared to you."

"And?"

"You've always won."

Amanda finally looked at Lucas. Her vulnerable expression matched his own. "This is a new step for us."

"How do you feel about it?" His voice was high and
scared.

"I'm not sure." Gentle fingertips smoothed the frown
from his mouth. "Right this minute, I'm not sure about
anything."

Chapter Eight

"COWARD!" Amanda was just about to make an ugly face in her dresser mirror but found she didn't have to. Her reflection was hardly complimentary. Dark pockets of flesh framed lackluster eyes, frown lines etched her mouth, an invisible weight rounded normally square shoulders—all indicative of a sleepless night.

From the sounds that emanated from Lucas' room, he too had spent the night in something less than restful slumber. Lights had gone on and off, footsteps echoed against the teak floor in the hallway, shadows moved beneath the transom.

Collapsing on the edge of her neatly made bed, Amanda stared at her hands, sweaty fingers twisting aimlessly together. This morning she had stayed in her room feigning sleep, deliberately missing breakfast and avoiding Lucas. She hadn't known what to say. She just couldn't face him.

Last night a new door had been opened. But was it the right door? Their relationship had always been free, easy, honest, secure. A bit of heaven. Had that all been destroyed? Would that one kiss spoil everything they had shared?

Damn! She just couldn't sit and mope all day. Get busy, get involved. Work it off. Maybe she'd contribute to the growing stack of firewood in the backyard!

Instead, Amanda watered the window garden, turning the thriving plants so all sides could bask in the warm sunshine. She ran a dustrag over the furniture, straightened lampshades, vacuumed the new carpets, trying to get motivated.

By noon, a modicum of energy had been restored and Amanda decided to head to a nearby suburban shopping mall. Purse slung over her shoulder, newspaper in hand, she opened the front door and backed into Wade Lloyd.

"Whoa." His arms slid around her waist, hands locking over the knot of her front-wrap denim skirt. "Slow down, Amanda." His affable grin filled her vision. "The afternoon was much too beautiful to spend indoors, and I remembered your enthusiasm for picnics, so . . ." Wade lifted the wicker hamper that was sitting on the front step.

Amanda's feelings were a mixture of annoyance and flattery. Spontaneity was exciting, but so was courtesy—she had always found the latter more endearing. "This is quite a surprise." Her hands made confused gestures. "I . . . I was just on my way out."

"What could be so urgent that it couldn't be put off until tomorrow?" his deep voice cajoled. "I had the deli pack a very special lunch. Pita sandwich pockets overflowing with rare roast beef, a sample of gourmet cheeses, fresh green grapes, giant strawberries and chilled French Columbard."

Wade's vibrant blue eyes rivaled Nature's tinted sky; his knuckles flowed along the curve of Amanda's jaw. "Why don't you exchange your blouse and skirt for a bathing suit and jeans. We'll saddle the horses and adjourn this discussion to the pond."

Her lips curved into a smile. "I think you've made me an offer I can't refuse." Her hand patted the green alligator on his blue knit shirt, teasing the hard nub of a masculine nipple.

Buttercup was skittish of her new rider. Amanda had to dismount Maizey, grab the other horse's curb bit and cheek strap, which finally enabled Wade to mount. "I think she can tell I haven't done this in a while," he said and laughed, settling a bit uncomfortably into the saddle.

"Nonsense. You have a natural seat." Amanda's serious tone belied the laughter in her eyes. Her heels cued Maizey down the well-worn trail to the pond. Randomly, she turned back to check on the much slower progress of Wade and Buttercup.

This was a different Wade Lloyd. Gone was the perfectly tailored business suit, professional manner and luxury car. In their place was a blue jean and sport shirt man, slightly unsure of himself and this type of horsepower.

Amanda found she liked the vulnerability he was exhibiting. The rigid shell was broken, the real man was exposed. A smile lightened previously pensive features. She was very glad Wade arrived today. She liked him, but she was also aware that being with Wade was infinitely less complicated than thinking about Lucas.

The glasslike pond mirrored the sky, a rich blue with dollops of whipped-cream clouds. "This was worth it." Wade dismounted. He took a deep breath, stretched and relaxed stiff muscles that hadn't been used in years.

"The water temperature is a bit chilly," she advised, tethering the horses and unbuckling the backpacks that carried their luncheon supplies.

"I'm game." He stripped off his clothes, his athletic physique emphasized by snug-fitting white swim trunks piped in navy. "Coming?" Wade held out his hand.

The picnic blanket was tossed under a tree, the packs carefully set aside. Amanda pulled the emerald terry shirt over her head and stepped out of her jeans. Her supple figure encased in a burgundy leotard that did double duty as a swimsuit, the keyhole-style neckline accentuating full breasts.

Hand in hand, five running strides sent the laughing couple splashing in the brisk, waist-deep water. "You weren't exaggerating," Wade said and shuddered, lifting his arms for her inspection. Goose bumps sprang amid the dark, curly hair.

"You poor thing," Amanda cooed, her expression totally guileless. She insinuated herself between his arms, hers lifting in an embrace, but the palms that rubbed his broad chest were filled with icy liquid.

He caught her hands, holding them tight against his hair-roughened torso. They became warm under his body heat. "You are a rascal." Blue eyes glittered a momentary warning.

She took a deep breath, waiting for the expected dunking but found instead her mouth covered by a more provocative form of moisture. Wade's lips were gently persuasive, his tongue teased hers. They played a skillful duel. Intimate foils engaged in masculine thrusts and lunges against feminine parries and ripostes.

Amanda's toes burrowed into the firm mud, glad of the sobering ripples that washed against her legs. "I think we're making the water boil," came her sultry murmur, hands cradling his face.

Wade's fingertips zigzagged an electric trail the length of her backbone, finally settling low on her spine. "I missed you yesterday. What did you do?" His passion-dark gaze concentrated on her lips.

"Slept late."

"Dream about me?"

Her throaty laugh taunted and mocked. "I think the way to your heart is through your ego, Mr. Lloyd." Amanda gave him a rough push that sent him stumbling backward into the water. Turning, she struck out for the other side of the pond, becoming more refreshed and exhilarated. She wasn't sure if it was due to the energies expended swimming or the presence of her male companion.

Wade's powerful strokes easily caught up to Amanda. "I think you're leading me on a merry chase, Miss Wyatt." He shook the water from his face.

"I have the feeling you enjoy the excitement of the hunt," she parried evenly, drifting to float on her back.

His hand dribbled cool droplets on her swelling cleavage. "I know I'm going to enjoy the prize."

She laughed again, turned and quickly disappeared beneath the surface. Amanda caught Wade's ankles but was unable to topple him. He was smiling when her face reappeared. "You're like the rock of Gibraltar," she said. Her lips formed a pretty pout.

"Come on, mermaid"—his fingertip buffed the water off her nose—"I'll race you back to shore." He gallantly let her win, letting his gaze feast on a more inspiring trophy—the enticing curves of her buttocks that the wet leotard so effectively profiled.

Amanda spread the dark green Army blanket on the ground while Wade expertly uncorked the bottle of wine, pouring the crystal vintage into plastic glasses. Foil-wrapped packages were opened to reveal an elegant deli feast.

"This is delicious." She bit into a mammouth red strawberry, the rich juice running down her chin.

His fingers became a napkin, catching the luscious, pulpy liquid and transferring it to his own mouth. "Delicious," came his low echo. Wade's lips replaced his hand, tongue savoring the essence of Amanda.

Somehow she managed to wiggle a plump green grape to run interference. "You may find yourself getting a cold shower if you don't behave." Amanda smiled the warning.

"Can I help it if I find you decidedly irresistible." An overflowing pocket sandwich was slapped into his approaching hand.

The warm sunlight and the potent wine aided the fermenting of relaxed camaraderie. Amanda peeled the red wax that coated the plump circle of mild Gouda cheese. "What were you doing yesterday?" she inquired, handing him a slice of cheese.

The semisoft curds melted against his tongue, the wine cleansed his palate. "I shared open-house duties with Kitty at the Crestfall Condo project." Wade looked thoughtful. "You might be interested in one of the units. They make a great investment. You could rent it out or"—he cast an inquiring glance—"you might move into it yourself."

"I'm just here for a vacation," Amanda reminded him. "I do have a home in New Orleans."

"Is there a law that says you can't have two?" His hand curved around her kneecap. "I already dread the thought of your leaving." Palm flowed along supple thigh. "I think what bothers me the most is your being here, alone with

Lucas." His finger pulled the elastic on the leg opening of her leotard.

If certain events and feelings hadn't blundered into the open last night, Amanda would have laughed off Wade's comment. "Lucas and I have known each other for twelve years; I don't think he's about to attack me." She tried to keep her tone light and humorous.

Wade gripped her arm. "I would kill him if he did." He pulled Amanda onto the blanket, his powerful upper body holding her captive. "This may sound insane. I've known you for only two days, but you've become very, very important to me, Amanda."

Swallowing convulsively, emotions in a turmoil. "I'm ... I'm flattered ... surprised ... I'm ..." She was babbling like a schoolgirl. Did Wade always move this fast? Or was this a new line she had yet to hear?

A soft smile etched his craggy features. "I didn't mean to scare you." The knuckles that caressed the sensitive cord of her neck were as gentle as his voice. Wade was anxious to calm and soothe, silently cursing his own verbal inadequacies.

A woman whose very existence he had never imagined had monopolized his thoughts since Friday night. Amanda had style, that enigmatic quality that comes from within and transcends everything else. True, he had been involved with more beautiful women, but somehow he found them lacking. Amanda ... she had yet to disappoint; Wade imagined she couldn't.

Soft feminine swells formed against rugged masculine angles. Her body was talking a silent language to his. "You aren't scaring me." Amanda's steady gaze radiated a lustrous sheen; her voice was like velvet.

"But you don't believe in"—he hesitated, then took the plunge—"love at first sight?"

"No." Her tongue circled berry-stained lips. "Infatuation, attraction, maybe lust." Amanda gave an encouraging smile.

Wade pressed his forehead against hers, noses rubbed together in an Eskimo kiss. "You are a very tough lady to convince," head twisted, his lips spoke persuasively against hers, "but I'm definitely the man to do it."

Amanda became mesmerized by the stealthy advance of his predatory mouth. Hands and fingers performed erotic little miracles against her skin. He had a sure, easy touch that inflamed her inner vortex and inspired mutual reimbursement.

All-encompassing fire replaced icy sensibilities. Her hands moved across his shoulders and back, pressing into the working muscles. Ten fingernails became provocative instigators, carving invisible sensual squiggles that aroused and goaded.

Firm strokes massaged her thighs, deftly changing to light, teasing fingers that pattered over her slightly rounded stomach, wiggling into the indentation of her navel before sliding purposefully upward to capture a full breast. Wade's thumb slid into the keyhole opening, luxuriating against swelling satin skin and an urgent nipple.

Her even white teeth gave a warning nip against his consuming mouth, breaking the connection. She wasn't a tease, she wasn't testing. Amanda didn't know quite how it happened, but things were getting slightly out of control.

A suffering growl escaped Wade, warm lips pressed a final kiss to her exposed cleavage. "Amanda, I'm sorry, but you're far too tempting a morsel."

Her hand came up to ruffle her damp curls. "I'm sorry, too. I wasn't trying to tempt." A low laugh escaped, and Amanda softened her refusal. "I think I'll have to reread that book I bought on body language. I must have mistakenly shifted into a wrong position."

His sapphire eyes rivaled her diamond irises. "Maybe I was just being premature."

"Why don't we get back to our picnic." Amanda reached into the backpack for a plastic-lidded bowl. Sweet cubes of watermelon restored the carefree mood. Ruby-red fruit was refreshing, and the slippery black seeds were tossed back and forth in a playful game.

"Where were you off to when I stopped by?" Wade inquired, splitting the last of the wine between them.

Amanda had to stop and think. "Just shopping, nothing important."

He looked at his gold watch. "Why don't we head back, shower, change and I'll take you for that shopping trip and we can have dinner."

"You are a man of great ideas, Mr. Lloyd."

"I'm a man who knows what I want, Miss Wyatt."

Lucas was pacing the back patio, right fist smacking against left palm. Business suit had been exchanged for denims and a sport shirt, both speckled with wood chips. When the pounding of horses' hooves assailed his ears, he swallowed his temper, managed to project a calm, friendly façade.

"Hello, Crosse," Wade said as he reined in Buttercup and gamely dismounted. He extended his hand. "Think you'd been ravaged by rustlers?"

Lucas' strong fingers issued a punishing greeting as he stared at Amanda. "Not at all. I have complete trust in my house-" Lucas was about to say "guest" but decided on a more possessive word: "mate."

Amanda slid off Maizey, fingers fluffing out matted, sun-dried curls. "You're home early, Lucas." She successfully hid the amusement in her voice after noticing his clothes bore the unmistakable and increasingly frequent imprint of the woodpile.

"I had some important things to clear up at home." Lucas' hazel eyes favored her with a meaningful glance.

"Since you're going to be occupied with business tonight," Wade inserted, flexing the fingers on his right hand, "you won't mind my taking Amanda out shopping and for dinner."

Lucas sucked in his cheeks and was about to make a rude counterstatement when Wade smoothly put both horses' reins in his hand. "I know you'll want to cool down your horses." He turned to Amanda and smiled. "Why don't we get ready."

If I had any pride and intelligence at all, Amanda thought, *I would leave these two rams to lock their horns in battle over some other ewe.* But this was one of those times to say nothing, to flirt and enjoy and to let events direct themselves.

All this attention was new to Amanda. She found being the focal point in a *ménage à trois* quite exciting. Vanity defeated pride. She gave Lucas a brilliant smile, slipped her hand into Wade's and led him into the house.

"He doesn't look very pleased." Wade looked back over his shoulder at Lucas' statuelike posture.

"Nonsense," her voice was bubbly, "he's probably thinking about some legal problem." Amanda directed him down the hall. "Why don't you use the bath in Lucas' room. I'm sure he won't mind."

Wade nodded. "Just let me get my things from the car."

The minute the front door was closed, the patio doors were opened. A tall, commanding figure stalked into the room. "All right, Mandy," Lucas all but growled, "what's going on? What the hell is he doing here?"

Leaning against the back of the sofa, legs crossed at the ankles, she projected a look of innocence. "We went for a picnic by the lake."

"*Our* lake." He looked hurt. "Now, that was crude!"

Amanda laughed and shook her head. "Come on, Lucas, the guy arrived, picnic hamper in hand. What was I supposed to do?" She looked down at her sneakers. "Besides, I like Wade."

"Wonderful!" His hand slapped his thigh, he took a deep breath. "Am I to assume this is going to be a duel at dawn?"

Startled, she looked up. "Lucas, are you saying . . . are we going to . . ."

A pair of very proprietorial hands gripped her upper arms. "I've spent most of the day rehearsing this great little speech, only to come home and find my audience missing." Lucas' hazel eyes were flecked with more green than normal. "I thought the two of us might begin at the beginning. I even brought flowers." He nodded toward the coffee table.

She turned, gray eyes softening on a crystal vase that held a dozen pink rosebuds. "Lucas," Amanda's hand caressed his jaw, soothing the harshness, "that was so—"

The front door was opened, and Wade's cheery whistle obscenely cursed their privacy. "There you are, Lucas. Those horses of yours are munching your geraniums." He cast a stern eye to Amanda. "Come on, darling, hadn't we better get a move on?"

Duel at dawn. Amanda pushed away the proddings of her conscience and allowed herself a happy smile. Her glow had nothing to do with cosmetics. This chain of events certainly had not been on her vacation schedule. In fact, never in her wildest dreams had she envisioned these circumstances. She made her way back to the guest room.

Two men! She applied double daubs of Gloria Vanderbilt's heady perfume to all her body pulse points. A major point in all this, she acknowledged with a grateful prayer, was the fact that she and Lucas were communicating—if somewhat dramatically! Gone was that initial awkwardness she had felt that morning.

Lucas. Amanda slid a burnt orange cap-sleeve silk shirt over her head and tucked it into a midnight blue challis skirt. They had a friendship that suddenly caught fire. She found the prospect of getting into a physical relationship with Lucas quite stimulating.

Wade. A narrow gold belt was wrapped eight times around her slender waist, adding a bit of gilty glamour. To be truthful, Amanda liked him equally as well. He was new, exciting, fascinating, yet comfortable.

She sat on the edge of the bed, fitting low-heeled black pumps over stocking-clad feet. The narrow strap and gold buckle blurred, looming complex and impossible to fasten. Amanda took two deep controlling breaths and closed her eyes.

You are not being a tease. You will not be a tormentor. All you're trying to do is deal honestly with both men. She grimaced. Quite honestly, she was confused!

* * *

The suitors were seated on opposite sides of the coffee table. Lucas was on the sofa, Wade on the love seat; each man's gaze was fastened on the rose-filled vase.

Amanda's colorful outfit caught Lucas' eye. "You look lovely," he said and smiled, pleased to have spoken first.

Wade stood up, his frown twisted into a happier expression. "That's an understatement. Where would you like—"

The door chimes made them all blink in surprise. Amanda was the first to recover. "I'll get it." Her heels clicked across the teak tiles to the foyer.

"Hello." Kitty Byrnes smiled a greeting, her eyes shielded by silver-lensed sunglasses. "Is Wade still here?"

"Yes, he is." Amanda stepped aside.

"My goodness, Amanda" Kitty said as she pushed up her glasses to form a headband against a cascade of golden waves, "you seem to be entertaining a full house." As her blue eyes surveyed both men, she hesitated for a moment before crossing to Lucas. "Hello, darling." Coral lips made an imprint against his cheek.

"Why, you were right." Kitty viewed her surroundings with amazement. "This place has certainly undergone a dramatic change."

Wade cleared his throat. "You wanted me?"

"Uh, yes." She flicked open her vanilla clutch. "You left your beeper at the office. I kept phoning here but got no answer." Kitty slanted an inquisitive eye toward Amanda. "So I took the chance and drove out." She handed him a pink telephone message. "Mr. Rafferty called. He wants to meet you in an hour at the NorthPark Mall to see those three vacant storefronts. He says he has to make a decision by Wednesday."

"Amanda," Wade folded the note, slipping it inside the pocket of his blue striped dress shirt, "if you don't mind, while you're shopping I'll show my client those properties and we'll have dinner later."

"Fine." She smiled her approval, ignoring Lucas' irritated expression.

"Lucas," Kitty's voice was an enticing purr, "why don't

I stay and cook us dinner?" She tossed her purse onto the coffee table, blue eyes fixed on the flowers. "These are lovely, such perfect blossoms." She smiled at her boss. "Wade, where did you ever find them?"

He gave a dismissing shrug. "I didn't. Lucas must have brought them."

"A client," Lucas lied evenly, "a grateful client."

"Hmm." Kitty picked a smidgen of lint from her turquoise linen dress. "Carnations are much more an appropriate flower for a man, wouldn't you agree, Amanda?"

Gray eyes shifted to the lovely pink rosebuds. "It's the thought that counts." Amanda's tone was slightly sad. Suddenly going out with Wade felt more a duty than a pleasure. She looked from Kitty to Lucas. Maybe it would be better if they had some time alone. She retrieved her purse from the hall closet and smiled at Wade. "I guess we're all set."

The architectural award-winning NorthPark Mall was filled with fresh flowers; its wide corridors were lined with paintings by local artists. Though none of the fashionable boutiques sold window shutters, Amanda was able to find material for valances. She chose a ginger on natural stripe for Lucas' room and goldenrod on natural stripe for the two guest rooms.

Neiman's drapery department was having a sale. Amanda placed an order for a walnut wood rod, matching brackets and rings and purchased patio panels in parchment with toast-colored geometric vertical print pattern for the kitchen's sliding doors. Charging the draperies, Amanda experienced a slight twinge of perverse amusement in shopping for Lucas while out with Wade.

Two hours later, she returned to the mall's west wing; Wade and his portly, cigar-chomping client were still discussing the rentals for the vacant stores. After shaking an effusive Mr. Rafferty's greasy hand, Amanda settled into a metal folding chair in an out-of-the-way corner.

"Amanda," Wade said with a rueful sigh, "he wants to have another look-see at the store in the east wing."

She gestured toward the two large shopping bags and bare feet that wiggled against the cool flooring. "Why don't I just sit here and wait."

"You don't mind?" came his urgent question, and after receiving a second affirmation, he pressed a quick, hard kiss to her soft mouth. "I'll make this as fast as I can. There's an excellent steakhouse on this level."

Amanda stood up, stretched and filled her lungs, trying to revive her shopping-weary body. Her eyes gave a cursory examination of an empty store, then slowed for a more exact surveillance.

She liked the fact that there were no ground-level display windows or gaping open frontage. The only entry to the store was through double shuttered doors, very exclusive, very unusual.

There were about four thousand square feet of actual selling space and a small staging warehouse in the rear for deliveries. Amanda took note of the additional fifteen hundred square feet of private office and showing gallery in the rear. The storefront bore a striking resemblance to that of her shop on Royal Street.

The businesswoman in her began to surface. Her designer's eye quickly added color, texture and furnishings: pale salmon walls, burgundy plush carpet and good-quality antique reproductions. Cheval glass mirrors, silver tea service and china cups, personalized service, European fashions, hand-crafted jewelry and one-of-a-kind accessories.

A heady mixture of fear and excitement throbbed in Amanda's veins. Her mind was racing through numbers, calculating dollar figures, balancing coulds and shoulds, weighing alternatives and contemplating sacrifices. There were a lot of unknowns—but Wade had the answers to some of her questions. Amanda rebuckled her shoes, found a pen and note pad in her purse and started a list.

"This wasn't the way I visualized the evening, Luke," Kitty's slightly nasal voice whined in his ear. "Didn't you like the dinner I made?" Her breast pressed against his elbow.

"The spaghetti was good," he said without looking up. He shifted in the recliner, juggling a legal-size pad and two lawbooks.

"Good? It was excellent." She bounced in front of him, and her tiny hands attempted to cover his work. "I hounded the chéf at the Allegro for his sauce recipe."

"I guess I just wasn't in the mood to rush out and shop for all those ingredients." Lucas gave her a game smile. "Kitty, I . . . I really have to do this."

"Luke," her soft lips formed a pitiful *moue,* "please." She managed to wiggle onto his lap, ignoring the sounds of paper being crushed and books thudding to the carpet.

Her turquoise linen dress had long been discarded, replaced by one of his dress shirts. Buttons were undone, giving an excellent display of bronzed skin; the only variances in color were the pink-brown nipples that poked an urgent invitation through the white cotton. "I feel very ignored." Kitty's hands slid under his gray knit shirt, fingers and nails making little electric barbs as they tried to ignite the cool flesh.

"I'm . . . I'm sorry," Lucas stammered his apology. He had tried, tried very hard to let this blond nymph arouse him the way she always had. But it was no good. Nothing. He wondered if he had become impotent. "Look, Kitty, I didn't plan on having to entertain company tonight."

She stopped nibbling his earlobe. "Company?" Kitty stared at him, blue eyes narrowing in disbelief. "You consider *me* company?"

He cleared his throat. "Just a figure of speech." Lucas tried to pacify her indignation.

"I don't think so, Luke." She pushed herself off his lap; her apricot French-cut bikini panties offered little in the way of cover to her rounded *derrière.* "You've become very distant and disinterested. I'm the type of woman who likes attention," Kitty shook back her thick mane of hair, "and lately I haven't been getting enough."

Her fingers stroked along his jaw, turning his face toward hers. "You are very attractive and one of the best lovers I've ever had. I'm going to miss you." Kitty looked at her watch. "I might as well get dressed. Can I make you some coffee? I think my jar of instant is still in the fridge."

"No . . . no, thanks, I'm fine." Lucas followed the undulating movements of her buttocks; still nothing. Instant—that had been the backbone of their relationship. Kitty always wanted things done immediately; she seized every moment. Her life was as freeze-dried as the coffee she preferred.

"I'm sorry that took so long." Wade ushered Amanda into the red leather booth in a private corner of the steakhouse. "Hungry?"

"Yes!" She laughed and pointed to the queen-cut prime rib that was listed on the menu. "With a baked potato, sour cream and chives and with Thousand Island on my salad."

Wade nodded approvingly and gave the waitress the order, making his a kingly portion. "Did you get all your shopping done?"

"Not quite." Amanda hesitated for a moment, then tempered her inquiry with a smile. "Did Mr. Rafferty decide on a storefront?"

"No." He exhaled an exhausted breath. "He's trying to set up another shoe store. He has a chain of thirty in the Southwest."

Amanda took a sip of ice water. "I would imagine he'd prefer a store with display windows."

Broad shoulders gave a noncommittal shrug. "I think he's steering toward the east wing. He'd have the only shoe commodity on that side."

Their salads arrived and, conversation halted under the mutual enjoyment of crisp garden vegetables and tangy dressing. Amanda patted her lips with an oversized paper napkin. "Wade, just out of curiosity, what is the rent on the west wing vacancy?"

"Twenty-eight hundred a month, plus a percentage of sales over a certain amount."

"I assume there are a few other hidden charges?" she persisted, passing him a basket filled with hot slices of French bread.

He swallowed a cherry tomato, blue eyes searching her face. "Why do I get the feeling this has suddenly become a business dinner?"

"As long as you introduced the word 'business,'" Amanda pulled out her note pad, flipping through heavily inked pages, "I do have some questions that need answering."

Wade was glad his prime rib was tender because Amanda's queries were tough. She wanted to know about decorating allowances, mall association dues, advertising and promotional requirements, maintenance and security fees.

Over coffee, he ended up jotting notes about her notes, and on the trip back to Lucas', Amanda added more questions to his already burgeoning list. "Are you really serious about opening a branch of Rags 'n' Riches here?" Wade queried, hand cupping her elbow as he guided her to the front door. Blessedly there was an absence of a porch light.

Amanda frowned, forehead puckering in silent contemplation. *Am I serious? Or has the idea been a momentary fantasy? I've never considered opening an annex shop, especially in another state. Would my present monetary worth support such an action? Would there be enough customers here interested in European fashions?*

Her left eye began to twitch against a stabbing pain, and churning sounds emitted from her stomach. Though Amanda was exhausted from the previous night's loss of sleep and bone weary from horseback riding, swimming and shopping, she instinctively knew insomnia would reign supreme. Seemed like old times!

Wade's hands settled into the curve of her waist. "Amanda, have I lost you?"

She gave a start; his voice came from a long way off. "I'm sorry." She shook her head, hands that held shopping bags lifted in a futile gesture. "I guess I was lost in a world of my own. You've given me something to think about." Preoccupied, Amanda automatically opened the front door and after a polite good night stepped inside.

Hands jammed into his gray trouser pockets, Wade made his way back to the car. This was not the way his evening was supposed to end!

The shaft of light that slanted along the hallway formed a guiding beacon that Amanda followed into Lucas' bedroom. "Hi! Did you have a nice evening with Kitty?" She placed the newly acquired draperies and material under the arched window.

"No. You knew that I wasn't going to." His chestnut gaze scrutinized every inch of her, much as an inspector checks for damages. "How was your evening with Wade?" Lucas placed his lawbook on the nightstand and elevated the mattress, giving Amanda his full attention.

"That client monopolized most of the evening. I found a few things and we had a nice dinner at the mall." She shuffled over to the empty side of the bed, sat down and unbuckled her shoes. "Lucas?" Amanda relaxed into the mattress, smiling as she felt the massaging action against her skin.

"What?" He came up on one elbow, sheet falling back to display a broad expanse of naked chest. Lucas studied her face, the closed eyes and the three vertical "worry" lines that radiated from the bridge of her nose. Gentle fingers tried to eradicate the strain. "Is Wade giving you a hard time? Is he pressuring you? If he is, I'll . . ." His tone changed from tender concern to barely repressed rage.

A low chuckle escaped Amanda. Without opening her eyes, she turned her head. "No, but I find it interesting he wondered the same about you." She smiled at his muffled expletive. "I was about to consult you in your professional capacity." Amanda's eyelids fluttered open, gray eyes alert with a brilliant burning.

Lucas consulted his digital watch. "This is after normal working hours, Miss Wyatt. I'm afraid my fee will be more substantial than a mere necktie."

"I'm serious, Lucas!"

"So am I."

She gave him an exasperated scowl. "I'm so desperate to pick that intelligent legal brain of yours that I'll agree to anything."

He rubbed his palms together and gave her his best leer. "You'll be doing your fellow man a great service. Kitty did her best to get a rise out of me tonight, but it was no go. We're no go. I want to make sure I'm not doomed to a life of celibacy because I have all these lascivious dreams about you and—" His erotic babblings were smothered beneath a bed pillow.

"Listen to me, Lucas Crosse," a peremptory index finger pounded a warning tap between his glittering eyes, "if you think you're getting any more than a good-night kiss out of me, you might as well pack yourself in ice cubes!"

He easily pushed aside the pillow. "Brutal but beautiful!" Lucas' fingers turned her scowl into a smile. "Go ahead, ask me whatever is on your mind." He settled back against the mattress.

Amanda switched off the vibrator and sat cross-legged, her back forming a barrier against his dominant masculine presence. "While Wade was finishing with his client, I waited in one of the vacancies." She cleared her throat and took a deep breath. "Lucas, it reminded me so much of Royal Street. The same layout, the warehouse area, two big rooms for an office and showing space. There were no display windows, very exclusive, very elegant—the look that's missing in the wide-open department stores.

"I . . . I asked Wade about the rent and all the other fees; he knew some and he'll check on others. I did some rough figuring, and looks like the initial investment would be around one hundred fifty dollars a square foot." She swallowed, turning her head to view his reaction. "The store has four thousand square feet."

Lucas exhaled a silent whistle. "Mandy, you're probably looking closer to a million dollars. You know how costs keep rising, estimates run over budget, there's always something that follows Murphy's law."

"I know. I know."

"I suppose it wouldn't hurt to do a cost study, feasibility

report, get estimates. Test the local banking waters, see what we find. You've got sound financial backing in Rags."

She fell back against the pillows. "Lucas, are you serious? Will you really do it?"

His wide, dimpled grin answered her questions. "Tomorrow soon enough?"

"You are marvelous!" Her hands cupped his smiling face. "I promise I won't be too devastated if you say this idea is economically unsound."

"That's a lie and you know it." His arms imprisoned her waist, holding her tight against him. Her sensuously smooth silk-covered breasts felt naked against his bare chest. The delicious floral scent of jasmine and roses silently encouraged a more reckless encounter.

"I promise. No tantrums, no tears, no grumps, no glumps."

The erogenous swells and curves that were Amanda revitalized Lucas' formerly gelded spirit. "I'll take you on your word." A blistering rush of heat turned him into an aggressive, excited stallion. "You did promise me a good-night kiss."

Luminous obsidian pupils were crescented by sterling irises. "I did, didn't I?" She pretended to ponder the idea for a moment; darkened lashes provided a protective shield. "It does seem fair that I give a good-night kiss to someone."

Lucas' broad chest vibrated under throaty laughter. "You're going to pay for that one, Mandy!"

Five masculine fingers pressed into her scalp and lowered her head. His greedy mouth feasted on full, half-parted lips; an eager tongue explored farther, sampling the sweet nectar inside.

A small sigh escaped Amanda, she relaxed and became a slightly shy participant. Her hands pressed into the tempered strength of his shoulders. Her exploring fingers moved lower, becoming lost amid the luxurious mat of hair that furred his chest.

Lucas' mouth became more demanding, raping and pillaging for his own pleasure, devouring the very essence of her. Calloused fingers ruffled silken curls in wild disarray, others purposely destroyed the protective straping of Amanda's gold belt, seeking to conquer the sensuously smooth skin on her back.

Passions collided. Starting like small ripples in a pond, they strengthened to a warm wash of waves until Amanda felt as if she were drowning. She could feel his body harden beneath hers; his intrinsic maleness prodded her pliant female form. Her fingers clawed against his heart, the erratic beat surmounted her own.

A new fiber was being woven into her feminine fabric. Amanda felt alive and womanly but somehow anxious and afraid. Physical intimacy was more than a mechanical act to her. Although she and Lucas were hardly strangers, adding a sexual exchange at this time might alter sensibilities, might take a still intangible 'something' and build into it an importance that might not be deserved.

Amanda struggled hard for freedom. For a brief second, Lucas' sinewy strength proved invincible; then he released her. "I . . . I think you've exhausted my supply of goodnight kisses for at least a week," she tried to keep her tone light but her low voice was shaky as she eased herself off the bed.

"Wonderful," Lucas called to her departing figure, "you won't have any left for Wade!"

Chapter Nine

"AND YOU'RE GOING to call Art Goldman just as soon as you get to the office?"

Lucas took a deep breath. "That's the third time you've asked me and the third time I've said yes." He drained the last of his coffee. "I will call your accountant, get your first-quarter gross sales and net profits, tell him what you have in mind and then hold the receiver a foot away when he screams."

Amanda gave him a quelling stare. "Arthur never screams," her lips twisted into a grin, "but he mumbles a lot."

When he reached for the percolator, Lucas found she had confiscated the pot. "Hey! I wanted another cup."

"You've already had two. Haven't you been hearing all the reports about caffeine?" Amanda held up his navy blazer. "Let's go, counselor. Have you got that list of rough figures?"

Long arms slid into satin-lined sleeves. "Were you up all night doing that?"

"Actually, I slept like a log."

"Didn't dream about me at all?" A hound-dog expression formed on his rugged face.

Amanda raised a perfectly arched brow. "Strange, but Wade wanted to know if I dreamed about him, too."

Lucas' dark gaze radiated a flintlike warning. "Better watch it, Miss Wyatt." He tapped the end of her straight nose. "Women who light both ends of a candle usually wind up getting singed."

Amanda's fingers walked up the lapels of his jacket to

tighten the knot in his cranberry silk tie. "I guess I'll just have to decide which one of you gets"—her steellike irises matched her tone—"blown out."

"I kind of like the sound of that!" His moustache gave a suggestive wiggle.

"Get out of here, Lucas." Amanda shoved him toward the patio doors. "Call me as soon as you hear from Art."

"Mandy, I do have other clients." He picked up the brief-case that was on the kitchen counter. At her little-girl pout, Lucas relented. "Why don't you drive into the city and we'll have lunch?"

"I'm wallpapering the kitchen and the hallway. I don't want to stop in the middle."

"All right, dinner. I know this great little French restau-rant—"

"French!" She smiled at him. "You've got a date."

At precisely nine o'clock, Amanda stopped wallpapering and reached for the telephone. Eleven musical beep tones later, Sherry Lau's gentle voice came on the line.

"Boss, you must have ESP."

"Something's wrong!" Amanda's suddenly moist palms wiped against her work jeans. "I can be back within the day." She silently cursed herself for conceiving a new store when the original was still such an infant.

"Take a deep breath, Amanda." Sherry's calm tone strove for tranquillity. "I was going to call today to tell you that we've had the best two weeks ever—just under seventy-five thousand in gross sales."

"You're kidding!" She stumbled against the barstool, falling into the seat. "I should go away more often."

Sherry laughed. "Sometimes you amaze me, Amanda. You have that magic touch. You know what women want before they do. You bring them an outer reality for their inner dreams. Your fashion wisdom is what's selling. The first batch of those silk shirts I ordered from Reuben has been literally inhaled. I'd like to order more. Make sure we create both the demand and the supply."

"Listen, Sherry, you aren't exaggerating those sales fig-ures, are you?"

"No. I've been sending a tally sheet every week to your accountant. He's thrilled."

"What's your long-range prognosis?"

"We're going into the May–June wedding season and the high-school and college formals. The gowns you ordered have been arriving steadily, and they are gorgeous. No duplicates. I'm putting a small ad in the women's section of this Sunday's paper. I had that artist friend of yours, Tommy Ryan, work one up. Very classy. Both him and the ad. We've had dinner three times."

It was Amanda's turn to laugh. "I'm glad you like Tommy. I have every confidence in you, Sherry. As a matter of fact"—she cleared her throat, the beige phone cord curling through her fingers—"I'm not quite sure when I'm coming back."

"Does this have anything to do with Lucas?" The voice sounded hopeful.

"Lucas and Wade . . ."

"Two men? Mandy! Confucius say: The superior man guards against lust."

"And," she continued as though she were deaf, "perhaps adding a Dallas annex to Rags 'n' Riches."

"No kidding! Do you really think you can make them abandon cowboy chic? Where?"

"There's a storefront in the NorthPark Mall. It looks just like Royal Street, Sherry. I've never been enthusiastic about mall shops, but this one is very, very different." Amanda smiled slightly. "It's me."

"Then go for it. Confucius also say: What is right will follow."

"Sherry, would you like me to tell you where you and Confucius can put your little witticisms?"

"Now, now. A superior man is satisfied and composed." A bubble of laughter filled the phone lines. "Amanda, whatever you decide, you know the entire staff will back you. I can even work out a schedule so that we can come help set up the store."

"Thanks. I knew I could count on you. I'll let you know how things go. Call me if there're any problems."

"Okay. Besides, I want to hear all about your juggling two men. I may pick up some pointers."

The phone beeped as soon as Amanda hung it up. Wade's low timbre vibrated against her ear. "Good morning. What are you up to?"

She looked down at her wallpaper-gluey T-shirt and smiled. "I'm quite elegant this morning, lounging around in marabou and satin."

"That's sounds quite enticing. I wish I could drive out."

Amanda frowned. Goodness, Wade had believed her! Would he believe bonbons, too? "Actually, I'm busy hanging wallpaper. Did Mr. Rafferty make a decision yet?"

"Oh. Uh." Wade swallowed his confusion. "Yes. He's taking the smaller storefront in the east wing." There was a pause. "Amanda, are you serious about a shop in the mall?"

"More and more," came her affirmative comment. "I just talked to my assistant manager and found we've done record sales in the past two weeks; the forecast is sunshine and greenery all the way."

"I better get answers to all those questions you had last night."

"Lucas is talking with my accountant and working up some funding approaches. I'll be getting back to you with more questions by tomorrow."

"We'll do it over lunch. I wanted to see you tonight, but I've got a business meeting." Wade sounded anxious. "I seem to crave your company. Day and night."

Amanda ignored the not-too-subtle undertone of that last word. "I'll miss not seeing you today, too." That was the truth, no come-on. "Why don't we meet back at NorthPark Mall around eleven tomorrow. I'd like to inspect the place again and then we can move on to lunch."

"Hmm. That looks good. Think of me today, Amanda. I'll be thinking of you all night."

It took the BeeGees' *Saturday Night Fever* album to eradicate the sensual echo Wade's voice had implanted in her consciousness. Amanda diligently concentrated on her work. The wallpaper was smooth, seams practically invisible, patterns matched. She wasn't sure who or what was the speck of sand that would turn into the pearl. Lucas? Wade? A new store? Maybe even two out of the three? Maybe all three?

The phone beeped a greeting just as she sank her teeth into a second peanut butter and jelly sandwich. Amanda's hello was mumbled around a sticky tongue.

"Hello, Amanda? Lucas gave me this number. How ya doin'?"

"That all depends, Art," she told her accountant. "Were Sherry's figures right? Is there a chance for a second store?"

"The receipts match and there's a damn good chance you can expand. That's why I'm callin'. Lucas is sharp. We've been vollyin' suggestions back and forth all mornin'. I think you've surprised everyone with your business, Amanda. Projected gross sales look close, very close to two million."

A second bite of sandwich went down in one throat-scratching lump. "Doll . . . dollars?"

"Yeah! Whadya think? You've got a gold mine." A prodigious sigh came through the modular receiver. "Amanda, haven't I been tellin' ya for the past two years just how well you were doin'? Maybe now you'll listen."

"I . . . I just like to be cautious. Fashion is such a risky, competitive business. Clothes are a necessity, but fashion, fashion's a luxury, and that's what I sell, Art, luxury, fantasy, dreams."

"Apparently there's still a lot of people who can buy 'em. So enjoy. Let the Texans spend their oil dollars on your nice clothes." Art's voice underwent a change as his bantering was replaced by tough words. "Look, I think you can haggle down that monthly rental. At least give it a try, and don't go for more than 1 percent of the gross sales over seventy-five grand per month. Lucas told me what an ace act that mall is. Now about the initial financin'. I contacted Roger Mayberry, who handled your first loan. He's moved up to vice president, he pulled your account, was duly impressed and would like nothin' better than to have

Dallas dollars flowin' in to the New Orleans Savin's and Loan."

Amanda coughed, took a mouthful of milk and a deep breath. "Does . . . does this mean I'm . . . I'm a million dollars richer?"

"It certainly does."

"Thank you, Arthur."

"Don't worry. I charge double for handlin' the books on two stores."

"What the hell do you mean, 'It was all too easy'? Honestly, Amanda, sometimes I could cheerfully throttle you." Lucas looked over the top of the menu. His frown was directed both at his companion and the fact that the food list would need translating. "What the hell is *Pieds de porc St. Memehould?*"

"Grilled pig's feet, and can I help it if suddenly I'm insecure?"

"You've never had an insecure day in your entire life. You are a stubborn pioneer. I'm surprised that you're being so wishy-washy about this. *Le gigot qui pleure?*"

"Weeping leg of lamb. I'm not prevaricating, I'm trying to look at all the angles. Why don't you try the *steak au poivre flambé à la creme*—that's flamed pepper steak with cream."

"That sounds fine." With a sigh of relief, Lucas tabled the blackboard menu. "What are you having?"

"*Coquilles St. Jacques.* I'm homesick." That was a lie. She wasn't homesick; in fact, she had to keep reminding herself she wasn't home!

Amanda concentrated her attention on Lucas, watching the myriad facial expressions as he studied the small, red leather-bound wine booklet. He had come singing into the house, swept her off her feet and whirled her around until they both fell onto the sofa.

"Well, baby, looks like you're goin' to become a Texan." Lucas had laughed, nuzzling her neck with his bristly moustache. "I think I'm more excited than you are. I can't tell you how glad I am that you'll be staying."

How long could she keep staying with Lucas? She'd have to find a place of her own. She had mixed emotions about that, too. When she had first thought about leaving Lucas, it meant she would be going back to New Orleans. Now leaving would be moving to a furnished apartment or a sublet. She had grown accustomed to the natural wonders of ranch life.

Of course, she rationalized, having her own place equaled more freedom. She could entertain Wade, see if their relationship was going to continue, mature, blossom. She could also entertain Lucas the way she entertained other dates but on a slightly more glamorous, romantic note. No more T-shirts and denims, hot dogs and beers—that scarlet halter-necked toga had yet to be worn, and she loved using scented candles for a centerpiece instead of flowers.

"How about Tavel?" Lucas returned the wine list to the decorative metal holder that held the salt and pepper. "A rosé should serve both our dinners." When he didn't get a reply, he picked up the decorative amber candle, letting the soft glow silhouette Amanda's face. "I thought I'd misplaced you."

"I was just thinking."

"That's only natural. You're headed for an exciting new challenge." His hands gripped hers. "I am just so proud of you, Mandy. What an incredible businesswoman you are! I'll tell you honestly that Art floored me with those numbers today."

She gave a low, appreciative laugh. "I'll be honest with you, Lucas. Art floored me too. I've been so close to the business that I couldn't see its worth. When he said the bank was willing to back me with a million-dollar loan . . . I . . . I . . ."

"It seems you've been ignoring your own worth." He lifted her hand. His lips pressed a warm kiss against her palm, teeth nipping a love bite into the fleshy mound by her thumb. "How long has it been since anyone's told you just how perfect you are?"

Amanda became lost in Lucas' eyes, transfixed by the

candle flames that leaped in the infinite pupils. His husky
baritone stirred hidden feelings beneath her calm resolve.
His words of praise fueled her spirit, made her feel able to
conquer the world.

Lucas had always been able to make her feel content, relaxed and renewed. He offered stability, security and support. He allowed her to wallow in a modicum of self-pity
and depression, then made her see the funny side of life.
Amanda was so engrossed in studying Lucas Crosse that
she had to be reminded to eat her dinner.

The Café Brioche was a tiny, hole-in-the-wall restau-
rant, but the cooking was reminiscent of the French coun-
tryside, homey, flavorful and satisfying. Posters of Paris,
the Folies and the Louvre hung side by side with Impres-
sionist prints of Monet, Renoir and Degas. All were placed
to cover cracks in the rough-hewn plaster walls.

The fruit tarts that Lucas ordered for dessert were filled
with fresh raspberries under a currant glaze and topped
with sweetened whipped cream. Amanda detected a hint of
ground almonds in the delicate pastry crust. The espresso
was aromatic and rich, hardly the delicate finale that the
tiny little cups led one to believe.

"That was a lovely dinner, Lucas." Amanda relaxed
against the leather bucket seat of the Fiat. "That restau-
rant reminded me of that little café on the Boulevard
Saint-Germain by the School of Fine Arts."

"I know. I go there every so often for lunch."

She turned her head, her lustrous gaze flowing along his
rugged profile, harshly defined by the low green lights of
the dashboard. "I remember you being a meat-and-
potatoes man. Don't tell me you can function all afternoon
on spinach crepes!"

"Their quiche weighs a ton."

"Liar. That chef was superb." Her hand tugged against
his suit jacket. "Lucas . . ."

"Oh, all right, Mandy," came his sighed confession.
"Sometimes I got a little homesick for Paris. I let myself go
back in time, back to that lovely week we spent together."
Lucas slowed the car as he allowed his hand to leave the

steering wheel, fingers caressed her face. "I could never understand why until now."

Five virile fingers continued to explore her features; blind, calloused tips became sighted messengers to Lucas' brain. They pressed along the subtle curve of her cheekbone, teased apart her lips, nails clicking against teeth, tenderly pawing her tongue.

He briefly cupped the stubborn pointed chin. Fingers moved to flow down her throat until they encountered the large flat buttons on her black cotton jacket-styled blouse. Lucas hesitated for only a second, then proceeded to release the decorative barriers. With each abandoned fastening, a door opened, allowing Lucas closer contact with the warm, sweetly scented skin he was seeking.

Amanda caught her breath but said nothing, mesmerized by the erotic stimulation his exploring fingers provided. They traced the line of her lace-edged, satin-cupped bra, pulling at the small rosebud that highlighted the valley between her breasts.

His fingers provoked gentle friction against the velvety swells, moving down to tease the nipple that vainly tried to push through its satin bonds. The car weaved, sending Amanda, who was not using a seat belt, sliding against the door.

"I . . . I think you should keep your mind on your driving, your hands on the wheel and your eyes back in your sockets." Her voice was as shaky as her nerves. Amanda retreated to a nearly fetal position curled against the locked door.

Lucas understood the turmoil she was going through —he was experiencing the same himself. He made that the last caress, verbal and physical, for the night.

"Now, look, Amanda," Wade said, trying to tease her out of her growing impatience, "the rent is set. There's no room for negotiations. I've already given you the 1 percent factor and an eight-dollar-a-square-yard carpet allowance, plus paint and painters. That's all you're going to get."

"I've talked to some of the other merchants, and their rent is less."

"They've been here longer. Do you want this place or not?" He decided on the hard sell. "I have others who are interested."

Amanda turned around, eyes glinting with laughter, pen trophied between her fingers. "Where's the dotted line?"

"You are one tough lady." Wade's voice was tinged with admiration. He produced the required papers, using his leather portfolio as a writing surface. "I cleared my calendar for this afternoon. I thought we could have a private celebration party at my place, use the pool, the hot tub, relax, have a champagne lunch sent up, maybe dinner, maybe breakfast."

She signed the last document with a flourish. "Wade, that was sweet, but I only have time for a quick lunch. I thought we could go to that German deli around the corner."

"Wait a minute. What's the rush?" He found himself juggling multiple-copy forms, a pen and a suddenly cumbersome slim attaché case. "Can't you put Lucas' decorating aside for one day?" Wade sought to temper his anger.

Amanda neatly folded her copies of the agreement and slid them into her taupe shoulder bag. "I'm not working on Lucas' house today. I have appointments to select carpeting and paint, visit a local fixtures warehouse, talk with a carpenter and then—"

"All right, all right." His hands were held in surrender. "I guess I'll just have to be grateful to share a bratwurst with you."

Much to Wade's disgust, the deli had only counter space available. He draped his tan sport coat on the back of the metal stool and wedged his rugged frame onto the red seat. "Amanda," his deep voice whispered against her ear, "come on, cancel your appointments. This is hardly a place for a celebration."

Her knuckles caressed his cheek, chucking under his chin, hoping for a smile. "I can't. Really, I have every hope of getting the new store open in six weeks. By the way, you never gave me the keys for the security doors."

He half stood up, fished into the pocket of his brown slacks. "Here." Wade picked the white-tagged set and handed them to her, receiving one of the plastic-covered menus in return.

He stared at Amanda's profile, wondering if she were playing some feminine game with his emotions. She seemed to run hot and cold. At times he found it exhilarating, embracing the challenge with masculine enjoyment.

Blue eyes tracked the steady rise and fall of her full breasts beneath the sleeveless coral-toned crochet sweater, traveling lower where snug black denims zippered over a flat stomach, delineating the very essence of her femininity. The hand that held the menu began to shake. He had great plans for today, plans that would make Amanda realize just how much he cared for her, plans that would make Amanda totally his.

Irritation formed in his throat. He had never dealt with such a complex woman before. Amanda was very old-fashioned when it came to physical involvement. He found that intriguing. But she was definitely a new woman when it came to financial and business dealings. He found that scintillating. The more facets Amanda exposed, the more fascinated Wade became.

He gave the waitress an order for two reuben sandwiches, cole slaw and ice tea. "You know, Amanda, I would imagine you're going to be staying in Dallas for quite a while with the new store."

She stirred two sugars into her tea, squeezing the lemon against the side of the glass with a long spoon. "Yes." She gave a self-conscious laugh. "I hadn't really thought about it."

"You should think about moving into your own place, one closer to the shop. It would make your life a lot less harassed."

"Wade, I don't really know." Her finger pushed at the ice cubes that bobbed in the golden brown liquid. "I'm not sure I want to buy something permanent. I may decide to turn this new store over to a manager."

"You could rent," he persisted, his hand closed over her slender forearm. "In fact, there is a very nice sublet, fully furnished, in my condo. Would you at least take a look?"

"Let . . . let me think about it." Amanda smiled at his eager expression. "Right now the new store is number one on my mind."

Wade leaned closer, and his mouth whispered against her ear. "As number two on your mind, I'm definitely going to have to try harder!" His teeth sank a gentle love bite into the soft skin beneath her lobe.

Days moved by with inordinate speed. Amanda became a consummate time budgeter. She worked mornings on Lucas' house, afternoons at the mall and evenings planning the next day's activities.

The physical activities proved more energizing than draining; emotional pressure was minimized when Lucas had to return to El Paso for a week and Wade attended a four-day convention in Los Angeles. Both men kept the phone beeping with late-night catch-up calls.

"I thought I'd find you here." Wade's voice caused Amanda to look up from an engrossed study of numerous rolled blueprints.

She gave him a cheery wave from her cross-legged position on the newly installed burgundy carpet that blanketed the shop's floor. "You're back early?" Amanda smiled as his tall frame, clad in casual tan slacks and an Izod navy knit shirt, moved to her side.

"I'm a day late." He bent down, fingers lifting her face. "So much for the theory that absence makes the heart grow fonder." His mouth pressed an urgent kiss against her lips, probing tongue seeking substance from the moist recesses that had eluded him for a week.

"I have missed you, Wade." Amanda ruffled through the vibrant lock of heavily gray-streaked hair that fell in a youthful feather across his forehead. "I could have used you to order around some incredibly slow workmen."

"That's not the kind of missing I wanted to hear!" Two steely arms pulled her up, crushing her in a savage embrace. "I missed touching you." His fingers roughly pulled the cinnamon T-shirt free of the waistband of her white cotton pants, hands kneading her supple skin, enjoying the satiny texture too long denied him.

"I missed tasting you, too." Wade's lips again sought Amanda's, nibbling and biting in unbridled restraint. He inhaled her scent; the soft oriental tones only increased his passion.

"Do you realize how you control me." His hoarse tone rasped into her ear. "Here I was at a convention, ignoring parties, ignoring other women, concentrating my energies on the days I had spent with you."

"Wade, I—"

His fingers stilled her lips. "Amanda, you must know by now that I am not able to handle any more on and off again where you are concerned." Sapphire blue eyes transmitted a warning message to her smoky gray orbs. "I want you to become part of my life, a permanent fixture. I realize you are totally involved in getting your new shop off the ground. I respect your commitment to your business. I just hope you'll be able to make the same type of total commitment to me."

Wade released her and headed for the exit. "I'll be waiting for your call."

Exhaling a futile sigh, Amanda riffled through the papers that were spread on Lucas' new dining table. Wade's words echoed heavily in the back of her mind, as they had all day long.

The telephone beeped. She jumped nervously, hesitating for a moment before walking to pick up the kitchen extension.

"Hi, Mandy. How's everything going?"

"Lucas," she said, relaxing into the counter chair, "everything is falling, either into place or apart. How are you doing?"

"I'll be coming home tomorrow, should be there at six.

Mandy," he took a deep breath, "I've missed you. We've got to talk. Get things straightened out. I don't think I can take any more platonic pleasures."

Amanda swallowed the lump in her throat. That stabbing pain was back in her eye, the scrambled eggs she had for supper were gnawing in agony against her stomach. "Lucas . . . can't you give me a little time? I'm . . . I'm . . ."

"I know, you're confused and busy. But I'm frustrated and in love. Mandy, I love you."

The words were said with such conviction that Amanda did the first thing that came to mind: She hung up the receiver.

Chapter Ten

AMANDA SNEAKED a peek at the digital watch strapped to the passenger's wrist in the seat next to hers on the plane. Lucas should be walking through the front doorway right about now. He'd be surprised and pleased at his newly acquired oak executive desk and tan leather posture chair that were housed in the alcove, and the dining-room furniture. He wouldn't be pleased with the note that was taped on the refrigerator door.

Dearest Lucas:

I'm taking a quick trip to New Orleans to place fashion orders. I'm not trying to delay our talk. I do need time to get things in order. Please don't call. I fed the horses.

Mandy

And Wade? Wade should be arriving home momentarily. He'd see the red light on his answering machine, rewind and listen to her voice recite the very same words, except for the horse feeding. He wouldn't be pleased either.

The only people Amanda had pleased by leaving town were the workmen. They had promised, on the heads of assorted sainted mothers, to finish constructing the display closets, install the six chandeliers that had arrived, and protect any of the furnishings that might be delivered in her absence.

How long an absence could she justify? Amanda had agonized over that longer than she had in composing the mes-

177

sages to both men. She had finally decided on ten days: seven to complete her business, three to try to decide her future.

A chuckle escaped her. She was doing it again. Allowing her business to rule her personal life. The bald octogenarian in the next seat gave her an odd look before going back to the in-flight magazine's crossword puzzle. Amanda turned toward the window, eyes preoccupied by darkness illuminated by a few Christmas-colored wing lights.

Maybe that was she. Maybe that would never stop. Her business had always been an integral part of her fiber. In it she found joy and happiness and power. Why should she abdicate such a lovely throne? Shouldn't the man in her life want to share that too?

"Welcome home!" Sherry Lau embraced her employer with sisterlike affection. "You look . . . tired." Almond eyes assessed unusual ashen features, dull eyes, and a slightly wrinkled turquoise raw-silk dress.

"Thanks, I needed that!" Amanda deliberately ruffled her sleek blue-black cap of hair. "I'm going to camp out in my office and put through some orders for the new shop. Will you run interference?"

"No one will get back there. Not customers, sales reps or handsome men."

"Especially the latter." Amanda gave her a rueful grin before heading back into the tranquil environment of her design studio.

Settled behind her desk, Rolodex waiting to transport her to Seventh Avenue, Paris, Rome, London and Japan, Amanda took a deep breath, wished for a crystal ball, and went over the edge of dissolution into excitement. The struggle to thrive in this risky, competitive fashion world injected new vitality and strength into her soul.

Every year the fashion industry grew more diverse and more complicated. It was a world in which furs and woolens were bought in the sweltering heat of May and June; bathing suits and cottons purchased in the frigid winter. Piracy flourished, high fashion was full of apparent contradictions, and the American woman would no longer tolerate a closet of clothes that were designed to become obsolete.

As a designer she had tried to stimulate clients' appetites; as a buyer she tried to discern her customers' likes and dislikes; as a businesswoman she tried to make sure both efforts succeeded so she could continue again the following year. Now Amanda found she was at the helm of a new ship, sailing in uncharted waters. Like Columbus, she knew the world was round . . . but there was just a slight chance it was flat and down she'd fall.

Amanda was, as usual, warmly received by the various design houses. She had decided to order fall merchandise, buying things women could find only in her store. She made additional purchases of cruise and resort wear—Texas adjoined Mexico. Acapulco, Cozumel, Cabo San Lucas—those resort areas would be popular vacation spots for her new clientele.

Jewelry was ordered from French Quarter artisans: hammered silver and gold, goldstones, lapis, and scarabs—unique, numbered pieces that elicited second glances. Scarves and hair accessories were included, as were novelty items such as socks, jeweled stockings, incense sticks and sachets.

Loungewear for day and for night was next on Amanda's list. She ordered the unusual: sheer, innocent camisoles and petticoats accented with winsome ribbons of satin and lace: elegant, naughty bustiers and teddies that were meant to form a barrier between a woman's soft skin and her crisp business suit.

Leather and lace, silk and suede—such dichotomies formed the basis of her purchases. Textures and fabrics that were striking in contrast, just as were most women.

Business took only four days. Amanda worked overtime, the phone bill would be enormous, she prayed the results would be too. Her mind focused on her major problems—Lucas and Wade.

Amanda pushed herself out of the graceful Georgian armchair. Bare feet shuffled through mute gold carpeting, then she dropped face down on her crisp white eyelet bedspread. She rolled over, kimono robe twisting beneath her body, to stare in confused contemplation at the pistachio walls.

Wade's face loomed with three-dimensional accuracy. The shaggy hair, more gray than black, blue eyes that matched the easy smile, the age lines that only made him more attractive. There was no doubt she found him sexually exciting, and although Amanda had never consummated her passion, she had certainly acknowledged it.

At times Wade made her feel insecure. He was too positive, too fast, wanted everything right away. Amanda had held back little bits and pieces of herself, afraid they would be examined too closely, spoil the moment, burst the bubble.

When he had gone to the California convention, she had wondered about his fidelity. Wade was no boy. He was a mature man with desires of his own, needs that must be fed. She recognized that and found she was jealous of the unknown female who might do the feeding.

Did she love Wade, or was it just infatuation? Had flattery and attention disguised the heart of their relationship? Did they really have a relationship—one that would stand the test of time, careers, pressure?

Other masculine features became superimposed in her mind. This was a face that had spanned over a decade, changing and aging—along with hers.

Lucas. Hazel eyes that grew soft with concern or green with laughter. Brown hair that curled under perspiration and normally waved against a rugged profile. The long, rangy body that had broadened under physical exercise, the thick moustache he had hoped would alter the "cuteness" of his dimpled cheeks.

Theirs had been an unusual friendship from the very beginning. Platonic, brother-sister—but now they were man and woman, and those inherent differences had been explored.

Time and distance had never separated her from Lucas. Two bodies sharing the same mind, accepting each other's imperfections and laughing at them. She trusted Lucas implicitly, harboring no fears that another woman would enter his life for a brief encounter.

But was that love? Or had their friendship gone full circle—spiced with a dash of erotic stimulation that would burn out because they were truly only meant to be friends?

They wispy mosquito net canopy over her brass bed proved as intricate a web as her present predicament. Amanda spent the next four days trying to extricate herself, to pinpoint her emotions and true feelings.

"Hello? Amanda?" Masculine eyes searched the dark, nearly empty store. The only visible occupants were an elegant upholstered cherrywood chaise longue, a bottle of champagne in an ice-filled silver holder, two crystal glasses and a five-light candelabrum, pink waxed candles twinkling under gentle flames.

"Amanda?" the deep voice crackled slightly, a throat was cleared.

"Make sure the security gate is locked, please," she called, inspecting her mirror image one final time: hair tousled; makeup soft and subdued, gleaming skin anointed with rare, fragrant oils. Her only article of clothing was a scarlet toga; its elegant, one-shouldered drape was held by a delicate cord bow.

Suddenly shy and awkward, Amanda swallowed those feelings, banishing them to some nonexistent world. Tonight was a night built for truth, honesty and—a healthy dash of feminine wiles.

"I'm so glad you're here." Her bare feet silently glided across the carpet.

He cleared his throat, hazel eyes blinking rapidly. "I . . . I thought I might have misunderstood your message, gotten the wrong day, the wrong time." Lucas cleared his throat again, mesmerized by the shimmering fantasy before him.

"I made sure I called the right man with the right date and the right time." Her silky voice insinuated a subtle message.

"Wade. He's not . . . I mean, is he gone, out of your life?"

"He was never really *in* my life. He tantalized the perimeter for a while." Her hands moved invitingly up his torso, fingers gently worked the buttons free on his gray striped sport shirt. "I must admit I was flattered by the dual attention of two men. My vision was temporarily clouded and I couldn't see the real issue."

His large hands gripped her slender wrists, pressing her palms flat against his heated flesh. "What was the real issue, Mandy?" Lucas's dark gaze leveled into her eyes; his expression echoed the seriousness of his tone.

"A difference between love and infatuation. I must have been in love with you for years, Lucas. That's the reason no man was ever quite good enough. He couldn't be. I had already found perfection. I had already known my Mr. Right."

"I'm not perfect."

"Who is?" She smiled at him, and an aura of love seemed to surround her. "You're perfect for me, Lucas. You're kind, tender, supportive. You let me be me, you don't try to make me conform or change. I think I appreciate that most of all."

Amanda closed her eyes and took a deep breath. "We've enjoyed a very intimate relationship. Lately, we've both realized that mental and emotional intimacy is not quite enough. Physical blending is needed to complete the triad."

Diamond-bright irises made a provocative envoy. Her body skimmed against his virile length, issuing a silent, sinuous invitation.

"There's no turning back," Lucas informed her, a hoarse edge to his voice. "I've been in love with you since the beginning. I guess I was too stubborn to admit it. Maybe I just wasn't ready to give up my bachelor life." His finger lifted her chin, he lowered his head. "Although to be quite honest, I've been very married to our relationship for twelve years."

"Well, then," Amanda burrowed even closer, and her

womanly ornaments branded their imprint, "I think it's time for consummation."

A husky laugh escaped Lucas. "Here? Mandy!" His voice lowered. "We're in a shopping mall, for God's sake."

She shook her head. "Here, Lucas. I've set the stage. Champagne, candles, chaise. No one can peek, we're behind closed doors."

"I can hear feet!"

Amanda pulled his shirt off his shoulders. "Pretty soon, you won't be hearing anything but my heart." Her fingers fumbled with the silver buckle on his belt, then boldly sought the zipper of his trousers.

A small sigh of futility was issued. Lucas kicked his pants aside, removed his socks and shoes. Amanda's fingers sought the waistband of his pastel blue briefs, rolling the elastic downward in agonizing slowness. They moved on to caress delicately, and she explored his intrinsic maleness, marveling at the quick-responding hardness.

Lucas gave a low groan and took control. With a gentle tug the toga spilled to the carpet, forming a silken pool; the candle cast Amanda in an ethereal glow. She came to him. The friction of supple, silken skin against hair-roughened masculine flesh aroused an inner combustion that enflamed them both.

Her tongue blazed a trail along the sensitive cord of his neck to his lips, then hungrily darted into his mouth. Her hands pressed along his shoulders, his spine, reveling in the virile strength.

Lucas' kisses proved more savage than gentle, crushing willing lips, branding final ownership on her soft mouth. He pressed her tightly against him, fingers kneading firm buttocks, lifting her hips slightly to accommodate his intruding male hardness.

Amanda guided him backward, letting the wide chaise provide more comfortable support. They explored each other with hands and fingers, mouths and tongues, seeking and finding the erotic little nooks and crannies that made currents of pleasure.

"You're so perfect," he said. Her swelling breast filled

his hand; his tongue and teeth teased and nibbled the hardened peak.

She moaned softly as his mouth moved lower, planting gentle kisses against her stomach; his tongue fit perfectly into her navel. The coarse hairs of his moustache tickled against her sensitive inner thigh; the loving lash of his tongue probed deep within her womanly core, creating sensations that wracked her body in tortured pleasure.

Amanda pulled his head back to hers. "I love you, Lucas." Gentle lips forged the tender acknowledgment.

Suddenly Lucas pulled free. He lifted her hips to meet the thrust of his violent spirit. He entered her tenderly but deeply. They became one, completing the mental and emotional union with this physical fusion. This was no one-sided possession but a joyful merging of souls.

Her long legs wound around his powerful hips. She felt him move inside her, building a symphony of pleasure. Her own body vibrated, synchronizing its movements with his. It was a total bodily experience of excitement and closeness.

Fluttering, pulsating sensations were building out of control. In a momentary standstill of time, her passion erupted. A sob escaped Amanda, and her teeth sank into Lucas' shoulder.

He pulled her closer, the force of him growing faster until finally his body shuddered and trembled under the explosion of his love offering.

They were both breathless, hearts pounding in mutual intensity of a perfect arousal. Lucas nuzzled her neck, his lips placing a delicate kiss against her ear. "I love you, Mandy. You've been there all my life. I don't ever want that to change."

"Don't worry, Lucas." Her hands cradled his face, eyes feasting on his beloved features. "We're locked together for all eternity."

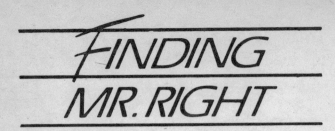

FINDING MR. RIGHT

Avon's new "Finding Mr. Right" series of contemporary romance novels each feature a heroine faced with difficult choices about her life when she finds the man who may not be quite perfect, but who is just right for her.

LOOK FOR A NEW "FINDING MR. RIGHT" NOVEL ON SALE EACH MONTH:

PAPER TIGER   February 1983
Elizabeth Neff Walker
An attractive, intelligent newspaper columnist is forced to assess her career's importance when she is pursued by two men—her good-looking editor-in-chief and a strapping outdoorsman. 81620-2/$2.75

DANCING SEASON   March 1983
Carla Neggers
An independent cafe owner must choose between a charming, world-famous ballet dancer and her older brother's attentive, easy-going best friend. 82602-X/$2.75

BEST LAID PLANS   April 1983
Elaine Raco Chase
Pursued by a dynamic real estate tycoon, a beautiful, vivacious boutique owner must reassess the importance of career and take a closer look at an old friend—a handsome, charming lawyer. 82743-3/$2.75

MORE "FINDING MR. RIGHT" NOVELS COMING SOON!

AVON Original Paperbacks

Available wherever paperbacks are sold or directly from the publisher. Include 50¢ per copy for postage and handling: allow 6-8 weeks for delivery. Avon Books, Mail Order Dept., 224 W. 57 St., N.Y., N.Y. 10019